CONTENTS

STERLING

BEARS OF BURDEN

CANDACE AYERS

LOVESTRUCK ROMANCE

Sterling Mallory likes fast—fast cars and faster women, anything to keep the ghosts at bay. Living life on the edge catches up to him when he carelessly makes an enemy of Kyle Barns. Who knew that Kyle's younger sister would turn out to be Sterling's mate? Now, his mate hates him.

Ophelia Barns left her flourishing journalism career in Nashville to come back home to Burden, Texas. Her brother has always been her rock, and now it's her turn to be there for him. When someone crosses him, they cross her.

When Ophelia is forced to interview Sterling for the local Burden Gazette, despite the fact that they don't have an easy time dealing with each other, the attraction is so intense that they might each be willing to make some sacrifices.

1

OPHELIA

Big and furry, I clumsily stumbled through the parking lot and away from the back door of The Cave with one foot stuck in a bucket. My bear grumbled and toppled sideways landing in a pile of leaves. Leaves and twigs stuck to my fur. I tried to sit up, but the massiveness of my midsection fought against the action. Tumbling to the side, I rolled onto all fours and forced myself to stand up on my back legs. Just because I was a bear didn't mean I had to be undignified. Well, actually, I was beyond undignified at this point, really.

I tossed one look back at the bar and shook my head. Yeah, I was way past displaying any semblance of dignity. I jerked my stupid stalker head away from the door where I'd been listening, and tried to watch where I was going as I tripped over logs and sloshed through mudpuddles. It'd been raining for days and everything was soaked. I wasn't a fan of mud. As human woman and a bear shifter, I didn't like having to clean mud from all my cracks and crevices.

I came to the swollen creek bed and roared—ooh, that was fun. I didn't want to get wet. Frustrated at myself for my own obsession that had driven me to the bar in the first place, I cupped my big head in my hands and rolled my neck back gazing skyward. Why couldn't I just let him go?

One way or another, I needed to get my big furry butt home, so I scanned the creek until I spotted a few rocks farther along down the river bank. If I could step from one to the other, I might be able to leap the last bit of distance onto land. That way, I could stay dry.

I was a complete basket case. Certifiable. There was no other way to view it. Take today, for instance. I'd been minding my own business heading home from work, what little work I had, when I caught *his* scent around the bar. I knew what he was doing inside there. I knew it, and the thoughts fueled my anger, which threw me into an uncontrolled shift and shredded my clothes in the process. Now, instead of being able to walk home along the sidewalks like a normal woman, I had to strategically cross a creek as a bumbling idiot of a bear, hoping I could maintain enough balance to keep myself from falling in and getting soaked.

I held my arms out to the side and snorted out a rough breath. I stuck my foot out when I noticed the bucket still attached. That wouldn't do. I stuck my other foot out and stepped on the rock. Gingerly putting my weight on it, I wanted to bellow a cheer. I wasn't going to get wet!

Luck disagreed. My weight pushed the rock down into the mud and the motion startled me. I lunged forward, trying to catch myself on the next rock, but the slipperiness of the slick, moss-covered surface sent me sliding into the cold creek. Water swallowed my growl as I went under and was swept downstream in the swift moving current.

I didn't even know if creek was the right word for the damned thing, anymore. It was so swollen from all the rain that it was more like a river. I came up sputtering, my clawed, furry mitts slapping at the water in frustration. I found my footing and stood up looking around to make sure no one was watching my performance in the shit show.

How had I sunk so low? I used to have it together. Now, here I was stalking men, stepping in buckets while stalking men, falling in rivers wearing a bucket on my foot while stalking men, and trying to make it home as the clumsiest, most awkward bear in existence. Hell, until coming back to Burden, my most embarrassing moment had been interviewing a popular country singer while unknowingly sporting a milk mustache on my upper lip. Once upon a time, I had my shit together.

I waded to the other side and dug my paws into the bank to try to heave my oversized ass out of the water. I ended up basically rolling in the mud. I stood up and kicked my leg out to shake the bucket loose. When it didn't budge, I roared loud enough to empty the nearby trees of any and all wildlife.

I would have shifted back to my human self, but I didn't want to risk getting caught so far from home naked. Of course, that would only be *slightly* worse than roaming around the woods as a frickin' bear.

I shook off as best I could and lumbered homeward. After a few steps, I stumbled and caught myself on a sapling, taking it down. I plopped on my butt next to the broken thing and snorted at it. I'd just killed a baby tree. I considered just sitting there for a while, until I looked up and noticed a bee hive in the distance. I groaned even as my bear took over, rolled to its feet and hurried toward it.

As human Ophelia, I knew better than to mess with bees. Bear Ophelia didn't give a crap that human Ophelia knew better and was struggling for control. I tried to fight the urge that drove me towards the hive. I was allergic. Not terribly, but enough to swell up painfully and look like a total alien freak show. I had very little practice controlling my bear, though, so she ignored me.

One big paw swipe took the bottom of the hive right off. Honey leaked out and along with it, swarms of bees. They attacked as I swatted and growled. Finally giving up the honey, I dropped to all fours and ran back to the creek as fast as my thunder thighs could move. I did a nose dive int the cool water and let it go to work soothing the sting.

My bear grumbled angrily at being deprived of fresh honey as I muttered to myself about the curse of being a bear shifter. I climbed back out when the bees were gone and lumbered the rest of the way home. There was some clumsy stumbling and another fall into mud, but I finally made it, leaving a dripping trail of muddy water behind me.

Kyle's truck wasn't in the driveway, so I shifted back to human right outside the backdoor and was finally able to shake the bucket off my foot before letting myself in. Kyle never locked his door. No one in Burden, Texas, ever did. It was slightly unnerving to me after having lived in a big city for so long.

I resisted the urge to inspect the perimeter to make sure no one had broken in. I was, after all, stark naked. I slipped inside and tracked mud and leaves all the way up to my bedroom. It was the same bedroom I'd had as a girl growing up in good ol' Burden. From birth to the fragile age of seventeen, my sanctuary had been framed by these four Pepto-Bismol pink walls.

I slammed the bedroom door behind me and headed to the adjoining bathroom. Climbing into the shower, I scrubbed myself until my skin was raw. Bee stings marred my olive complexion, and I could barely see out of my swollen eyelids by the time I turned the water off.

I got out and dried off avoiding the mirror. Throwing on underwear and slipping into a nightgown from my youth, I looked more like a granny than a twenty-eight-year-old, savvy, independent woman. But I had no one to impress. Ever.

Navigating the stairs carefully, I made my way to the kitchen and dug around in the medicine drawer until I found Benadryl. I popped three before retreating to the living room to watch an episode of *My 600lb Life.*

I was asleep before the intro finished playing. Nightmares of my mate flirting it up with other women plagued me and I woke up sometime later that as a 600lb bear atop a severely damaged couch frame.

2

STERLING

"Sweetheart, I will rock your world." I flashed the pretty blonde in front of me one of my signature cocky grins, and once again bit back the growl my bear tried to release. My bear didn't like this at all. Now that we'd found our mate, his instinct was to frighten away any woman I tried to callously and rudely flirt with. I'd be inclined to do the same if it weren't for the fact that nameless, faceless women were the only thing that filled the gaping wound in the center of my chest. And only temporarily at that.

"Aren't *you* sure of yourself?" Her face scrunched up like she smelled something bad and she took a step back, away from me.

"You're not gonna walk away from the best thing to ever happen to you, are you?" Inwardly, I cringed. Maybe I should start to dig deeper into my arsenal of cheap pick-up lines.

Her eyes practically rolled to the back of her head as she turned on her heel and stomped off.

I retreated to our table and sat down next to my older brother, Hutch, and our buddies. Three of them were recently mated. Only Sam and I remained single, and once Sam found his mate, it would just be me. Alone. I would be the last single bear in our close-knit group of shifters. I knew that for a fact—because I'd already found my mate and there was no way we were hooking up. She hated me.

"Ouch, that looked painful, bro." Sam grinned at me and clapped me on the shoulder. "I'm gonna have a go at her."

I watched him swagger off and tried to keep my face neutral. The impression I was going for was the goofy, slightly moronic, happy-go-lucky younger brother of Hutch. I was doing pretty well at keeping up the act. Still hitting on women, still pretending to leave with them, still acting like a jackass. I had everyone fooled—except Hutch.

Hutch looked up from his beer and shook his head. "What are you doing?"

I chugged my beer and stood up. "Boys, I've had my fair share of striking out tonight. I think I'm going to take a dip in the creek and head home."

Wyatt stood up. "I'll join you. Maybe if I do, by the time I head home, Georgia will be home."

Thorn's eyes were on his mate while she worked the bar. "I think it's time Allie's shift ended."

Hutch finished his beer and grinned. "I think it's time I fetched Veronica from her meeting. She should be done with her dirty book sharing by now, which means creative experimentation for me tonight."

Wyatt laughed. "Hell, I'll skip the swimming and just head over to the library with you."

I forced a grin and fit my baseball cap on my head. "Ya'll have fun. Don't do anything I wouldn't do."

Hutch caught my arm and raised his eyebrow. "You okay? We still need to talk."

I shrugged his hand off and felt the strain in my grin. "I'm good, bro. I'll be at the shop in the morning. The car needs some tuning before the race tomorrow night."

I slipped away and headed out to my truck. Backing out of the lot, I revved the engine before speeding off toward home. On the outskirts of town, my house sat near the top of a relatively small mountain overlooking the creek that ran through town.

It was a dark, starless night, and all I could see were shadows as I stripped out of my clothes and left them in a pile on my back porch. No matter, I knew the land like the back of my hand. I shifted and ran down the hill splashing into the cold water of the swollen creek. I dunked my head and came up with a big splash. My mind strayed, as it usually did, to Ophelia.

Thinking of her seemed to cause her scent to materialize out of thin air. It flooded my senses until my bear growled for her, hungry for more than sweets for a change. I listened, but there was nothing but the sound of the creek running and the crickets singing. I was just haunted by her.

I tried to distract myself by catching fish, but it didn't work. Having a mate and knowing she was nearby but didn't want anything to do with me, left me with a empty ache that invaded every inch of me and affected every aspect of my life. It was the worst pain imaginable. A year ago, I couldn't wait to find a mate, certain the entire experience would be fantastic. Settling down, having someone to wake up to, maybe little cubbies running around. Boy, was I wrong. Turns out that for me it meant one more person to disappoint. Hah! Not even to disappoint. I wasn't even being given the chance to disappoint. What I'd give to have her care enough to find me disappointing.

Surrounded day in and day out by my closest friends, as I watched them settling down, one by one, my heart ached as though pierced by the blade of a steel dagger. I hated the jealousy I felt whenever I saw how happy they were with their mates. They deserved their happily ever after. But damn, the jealousy ate me alive.

The thought of spending the rest of my life harboring this ache was a very real and constant fear. I'd spent more than a few nights staring at the ceiling, consumed with anxiety-driven insomnia as I dreamt of having the opportunity to shower Ophelia with compliments, with kindness, with little surprise gifts...with love. I didn't even know how to begin. It was all so fucked up. I'd messed up so badly without even trying.

My carefree, youthful, okay—*slime ball*—ways had caught up with me big time. I didn't think of them as slimy until I started seeing myself through Ophelia's eyes. I still put on a show for the sake of hiding my pain, but the thought of bringing a woman home who wasn't Ophelia made my skin crawl. I wouldn't do it.

I climbed out of the creek and flopped over onto the bank. I hadn't meant to make such a mess of things. I didn't even know I had a mate. Next thing I knew, I'd fucked up. The kicker was, at the time, I hadn't considered anything I was doing as being wrong. Sure, it was a dick move, but Kyle Barns deserved it. He was truly an asshat. Fuck, I'd done the whole town a favor by hitting him below the belt.

Sleeping with his fiancée, uh, *ex*-fiancée, a few days before their wedding was to have taken place, had completely blown up in my face. Kyle was the only family Ophelia had left, and the two of them were tight. Even though he was a giant dick stain, she loved him and I'd managed to humiliate him in front of all of Burden. Who knew his little sister was my mate? Before I'd even found out Ophelia was the one for me, I'd managed to not only alienate her, but also convince her that I was the lowest bear in the entire lone star state.

Tossing a furry arm over my eyes, I groaned. Even as a bear, the sound was clearly pained. I needed her to be happy. I wanted her more than anything. I wished I could be the one to make her happy, but I'd fucked it all up. By being me.

3

OPHELIA

The Burden Gazette was a two-page paper that could barely scrape together enough news stories to fill both the front *and* the back of its pages. In a town the size of Burden, even a die-hard investigative reporter would have a hard time uncovering enough interesting goings-on to warrant a newspaper. Karen was one of the old-timers in Burden, and she insisted on keeping it going. For that, I was thankful.

It wasn't the exciting journalism career path I'd been on in Nashville, and it certainly wasn't anything worthy of adding to my resume, but it was a job. Karen, an old hippie throw-back of a woman, the one who insisted on keeping the newspaper alive, hired me within minutes after I'd wandered into the tiny office to talk to her. She'd been doing all the research and writing herself and she was relieved to be offered a break.

I was paid half a cent a word. On a good week, I'd make up to a few hundred dollars. It was a mere fraction of what I had been earning in Nashville, but, again, it was a job.

To be fair, I wasn't sure how Karen was even able to afford to pay me as much as she did. The paper sold to a lot of the locals, but that didn't account for much. By the time she paid for the weekly printing costs and office space, I had to assume I was being paid out of her own pocket. On the one hand, I felt slightly guilty about that, but on the other, I had bills to pay. Student loans and insurance ate up just about every cent of my income. Without Kyle's help to buy groceries and such, I'd go hungry.

Despite it all, I liked the work. I found the gig quaint and charming in a weird way. Sure, the little Burden Gazette wasn't anything I could take too seriously, but memories of seeing my parents reading it when I was a little girl were still fresh in my mind. I pictured mom at the kitchen table, sipping from her favorite ceramic coffee mug as she devoured the tidbits of local gossip, and dad after work relaxing in his easy chair, feet propped on the coffee table, while scanning the same pages.

The fluff pieces I wrote weren't hard, and through interviews and such, I got to reintroduce myself to locals that I hadn't seen in over a decade. I'd left Burden shortly after Mom and Dad had both perished in a airplane crash. The accident happened just before graduation. My initial post-high school agenda had been to get a job in Burden, maybe save up some money for a few years before heading off to college. I had envisioned working during the day and spending my evenings curled up in the sunroom reading a book while Mom and Dad played cards. The devastating accident had changed all that. After my parents passed, I couldn't get away from Burden fast enough. It seemed everything triggered a painful memory.

I moved around for a while, and wherever I was, Kyle came to visit, so I never had to set foot back in my hometown. I hadn't planned on returning. Ever. But, as I'd learned at too young an age, "The best laid plans..."

A bad experience with a groping boss left me unemployed. At the same time I was fielding phone calls from Kyle who was having his own struggles over a breakup. In the end, I was convinced that it was time to face any demons that may be lying in wait for me back home. I actually wanted to come home again. At least for a while. It was my turn to be a shoulder to lean on for my brother, like he'd been for me for so many years. As my only living family, Kyle had taken on the role of my—everything. Anytime I was really hurting, he was there for me. I finally had a chance to return the favor.

Except, once I'd arrived in Burden, I learned that Kyle wasn't the same man he appeared to be when I was watching from afar. He had erected some sort of false facade. Saying his name in town often elicited grimaces and snarls from people. Kyle acted like a pig. There'd been moments since I'd returned when I wondered which was the real Kyle—the caring, kind-hearted man who had been my rock, or the piggish creepy Kyle. Which was the phony? Regardless, I figured I had to do my best to be there for him, no matter what.

The Burden Gazette was housed in the same narrow office it'd been in ever since I could remember, and it still held the same musty smell as I walked in. Karen, was sitting at her desk at the back of the room, like always. Round, wire-framed glasses with pink-tinted lenses perched on the end of her hook-nose.

Her face lit up when she saw me. "Philly! I have a job for you! I forgot to mention it before you left yesterday. The races start tonight. You know the old dirt tracks, right?"

My stomach turned over and threatened to toss the yogurt I'd eaten for breakfast. "Yes."

She wiggled in her desk chair, making it squeal. "Well, I want to do a piece on Sterling Mallory. He's rumored to be the top contender again this season. I saw him driving that fancy ride of his through town this morning and I must say, it's a beaut."

I gritted my teeth. "I can't do it tonight."

She frowned. "We've got nothing else to put on the front page this week, Ophelia. Unless you want that piece you wrote about the rank odor permeating the halls of Burden High School on the front page."

I could tell she was being a smartass. "It's a fine story."

"Sure. I've got the perfect headline:

Sanitation Hiccup Irritates Teens.

I can see it now. Great. Enthralling. Might even win you a Pulitzer."

I rolled my eyes and released a long, slow sigh.

"C'mon, Philly. This has been the slowest news week in Burden ever. I need the piece on Mallory. It's exciting. I've heard he's quite the lady's man. Maybe you can spin some of that into the story."

There was no way. Karen was pushing for something that she'd never understand. "Couldn't *you* do it?"

She shook her head. "I've got the trip into Dallas tonight. My daughter will be picking me up here this afternoon. The sleep study is going to figure out if I need one of those Darth Vader machines to breathe at night."

I closed my eyes and rubbed at my forehead. "Maybe I can find another, more interesting, story."

Karen's brow furrowed and I knew I was facing the stubborn side of the woman. "Do the story or I'll have to find someone else who will, Philly. I like you. You're the best writer this town has ever seen, but I need someone I can rely on."

I swore. I couldn't ask Kyle to pay my bills. "Fine."

Her smile slid back onto her ruddy face. "Groovy! I think you'll have a blast. Those dirt track races are so exciting. The concession stands have nachos and sometimes there's even a crash. It's really a good time."

I slid behind the desk she'd provided for me, and as I plopped down on the weird faux leather fabric of my chair, it made a weird farting sound that I considered a fitting response. I opened my purse and snapped the easy open Tylenol cap before shaking a couple out into my hand. I swallowed them dry and looked at the strange school smell article on my desk that I still wanted to run through once more for a final proofread.

"Take the camera. See if you can get a good shot of Mallory. It'll cost more to print, but he's quite a handsome fella. I bet a front-page photo will sell quite a few more papers."

I resisted the urge to slap my hand to my forehead. Barely.

4

STERLING

I dropped the hood of my car and zipped up the flame-retardant suit all the drivers wore. The races were a surprisingly big deal around here. The track was thirty miles outside of Burden and attracted drivers and spectators from all over. The dirt track was as refined as it could be and it was always a little rough on the cars, but I liked the edginess of it. Everything was a little more dangerous on a dirt track, and there was no telling what might happen.

I'd been practicing all day and I was ready to get on with it. There was nothing like speeding around a track, competing with other drivers to get my bear riled and distract me from whatever issue I was dealing with. Bears weren't meant to go that fast, but mine liked it, and I loved the thrill and thrived on the challenge.

I looked over the car at Hutch and nodded. "There's a storm coming in. They need to get this show on the road soon or we're going to be rained out."

He lifted his head and inhaled. "Still got about an hour. Enough time for the star of the show to drive his laps."

I laughed. "I'll pretend you're talking about me."

He grinned. "Try not to break anything too vital tonight."

"Now I know you're not talking about me."

"Hell no, I wasn't talking about you. You'll heal. The car won't."

I shook my head and leaned against the metal frame. A reinforced roll cage sat just under it, promising to keep me safe should anything happen. Being a shifter meant I'd heal from most things, but fires and explosions were an entirely different matter.

"I'm heading to the stands, little brother. Veronica is sitting with Georgia and Allie. No fucking telling what trouble those three can get into unattended for too long."

I lifted a hand in a wave. "Good luck."

"You too."

I looked around at the other drivers and inhaled deeply. I didn't normally get nervous before a race, but something had my hair standing on end tonight. The weather promised a doozy of a storm, but I knew it was more than that.

As a gust of wind swept over me, I immediately identified the source of my agitation. Under the pervading odor of motor oil and rubber, I could smell her. Ophelia. Her unique and delicious aroma, like whiskey and cupcakes, had my dick springing to life faster than I could reach down and hide it.

I muttered a curse and followed the direction of the scent. There she stood, across the parking lot, her wild hair whipping across her face. What the fuck was she doing here? Her sun-kissed threatened to swallow her whole, but she expertly yanked something off her wrist and had it pulled back in seconds. Too bad. I was sad to see it tamed. There was something about the unruly mass that made my heart race and my dick throb. That woman was made for me. Everything about her was pure seduction to every part of me.

As she lifted her head, her eyes locked onto mine. For a second, I let myself believe the parting of her lips was due to her hunger for me instead of shock at seeing me. Fuck, I wanted her.

I hadn't seen her in a few weeks and I'd missed the way the sun glinted off her olive skin and the world seemed to light up when she smiled. Ophelia never just blended in. No, she was like the north star —always the brightest in the sky. I wanted to run my hands over her, touching every part of her, but I shoved them in my pockets instead. I knew she loathed the thought of my touch.

To my utter surprise, Ophelia began walking toward me. Her posture revealed she would rather be anywhere else in the world and I could see her lips purse as she blew out a rough sigh. Still, she was coming over to me.

I stayed where I was but leaned against my car to keep from reaching for her. I kept my mouth shut, too, afraid to fuck up any more than I already had.

She stopped a few feet away from me and slowly lifted her eyes to mine. Her eyes—pools of silver-blue with a dark blue outer ring—threatened to melt me. "Hi."

I couldn't stifle a low growl at the sound of her smooth, velvety voice. I wanted to hear that voice as it lost control and cried out my name. Shit. I balled my hands into fists and closed my eyes. It didn't help. I could still smell her deliciousness, and still see her behind my lids.

My bear wanted to roll over and beg for forgiveness. Just expose our belly and throat in surrender—anything to win her over. I, however, wasn't giving him that control. Yet. I shut him up and opened my eyes. She was watching me wide-eyed.

"Hi, Ophelia."

She crossed her arms under her chest, a move which forced her cleavage higher. The little sundress she wore teased me more than any lover ever had. "I have a favor to ask."

I tilted my head to the side and furrowed my brows. I couldn't imagine what kind of favor she would ask of me. Maybe she didn't know it, but I'd move heaven and Earth for her, or die trying. The wheels in my head started turning. "What is it?"

Her wide mouth thinned and dimples appeared at the corners of her lips as she worked her jaw muscles. Her brows rose, and then squeezed toward one another. "I have to interview you. I mean, I'd *like* to interview you. The paper...well, *Karen*, thinks an interview with you would be worth gold for the front page of the Gazette."

I bit back a grin, knowing it wouldn't be well-received. "Karen wants *you* to interview *me*?"

She nodded and pushed a stray curl back. "Yes. So...whadda ya' say?"

I grinned fully then, unable to help myself. Her reaction nearly had me reaching out for her. Her mouth went soft and her tongue danced out to wet her lips. The scent of her arousal hit me like a blow to the gut. I couldn't stop the urge to tilt my head back and breathe it in, memorizing the heady deliciousness of her.

Ophelia's cheeks burned bright red and she took a step back. "Stop that."

I bit my lip and nodded. "Sorry. Yeah, of course you can interview me. Not here, though. After. I'm about to race and I need to focus."

She narrowed her eyes and her fingers started tapping out a rhythm on her arm. "Where?"

She was at my mercy. We both knew it. I also knew Karen could be one pushy old broad when she wanted to be. It was wrong of me to take advantage of Ophelia's situation, but damn, I needed every inch of advantage I could get in this situation. I needed my mate.

I'd been surviving with the assumption that I hadn't a snowball's chance in hell of winning her over, but I now realized that an attitude like that was defeatist. I'd never been a quitter, and I damn sure wasn't about to start now—not before my interview. I stifled a laugh and stared down at my sexy little mate. Tricking into spending time with me might be conniving and underhanded, but I had to leverage every opportunity. Besides, her arousal was encouraging. Maybe there was hope for me yet.

"Meet me at my truck right after the races."

She frowned, but nodded. "Won't you need to devote time to all your *adoring* fans?"

I ignored the bitterness in her voice and slowly straightened from where I'd been leaning. I towered over her smaller frame, but she looked up, meeting my gaze. "I'm more concerned about devoting time to my mate."

Her eyes darted around to see if anyone heard, then her glaring gaze settled back on me. "*Don't* call me that," she hissed.

I turned and walked 'round the car to the other side. I needed space between us to keep control over myself and my bear. "I'll see you soon, Ophelia."

5

OPHELIA

I huffed and puffed all the way to my seat. Frustration and bitterness fought each other for the chance to consume me whole. I was also sexually pent-up. My body was on fire and I couldn't erase the vision from my mind of Sterling, his head rolled back, a look of sheer ecstasy on his face, as scented my arousal in the air. It was on a reel, playing over and over again in my head. The man wanted me. I'd felt the heat pouring off of his body and couldn't miss the huge bulge in his pants that he'd shamelessly done nothing to hide. I wanted him, too.

I'd done an amazing job of avoiding him thus far. Weeks had passed since I'd last caught a glimpse of him. Not that he'd been trying to find me. He'd seemed perfectly content with the flooziest of floozies Burden and the surrounding areas had to offer. I was probably doing him a favor by avoiding him.

I realized I was growling and looked around to find that several of the people sitting next to me were shooting concerned looks my way. I forced a smile and faced the track. He was making me crazy.

I couldn't exactly help how my bear reacted. I'd never learned to control her properly. She wanted to latch onto Sterling and never let go. She wanted to roll around in his scent—bathe in it. I just wanted to run away. It was too confusing, this battle raging inside. No one had ever really explained the shifter mating call to me. Mom was a bear and Dad was a human. As far as I knew, they'd just fallen in love and had two kids together. The shifter trait hadn't even shown up in Kyle. Female bear shifters were much rarer than males, even in Burden, and I hadn't been around shifters in a long time. I'd never really learned about mates.

I mean, I got the gist. We were meant to be together, yada, yada, yada. Obviously, our fated mating didn't account for one of us being a horn dog who slept with everything in a skirt. I was better off not being with the man I was supposedly fated to be with. Clearly, mistakes had been made. What I couldn't deal with, however, was the incessant pull I felt toward him. Just seeing him turned my panties into a puddle and my body into a volcano, begging to erupt. It was hard to freakin' ignore that. I felt like I'd combust if he so much as touched me. I wasn't prepared for dealing with that.

I didn't know if it was possible to ignore the mate call indefinitely. If I managed to keep pushing him away, would I just go insane and wither away in a pair of damp panties? Maybe. The alternative seemed worse, though. Give myself to a man who couldn't help but be disloyal to me and wither away due to suffering daily heartbreak until death do us part.

I took a deep breath and sat up straighter. I'd find a way to do some research. Maybe there was something I could do to release us as mates—sever the bond. Until then, I'd just have to put a muzzle on my bear—and lock my knees together.

The races started and I was surprised to find myself leaning forward in my seat to get a better view. The cars were fast and loud as they rounded the track, and a fine mist of smoke and dirt washed over the stands. The roar of the engines was so loud that I couldn't hear anything else. There were a couple crashes—minor, but it didn't stop the heated exchanged between drivers afterwards.

I didn't see the car that Sterling had been leaning against when we talked earlier. It wasn't until half an hour later that I spotted it, and my heart tried to crawl up into my throat. My bear paced as she watched her mate face danger. Granted, the wrecks hadn't been bad thus far, but the potential was there, wasn't it? What if he got hurt?

Without meaning to, I stood and rushed down the stands until I was right up against the fence, alongside several children and teens. My fingers gripped the chain link, and I sucked in a ragged breath. I felt like I was taking a backseat to my bear's reactions and had to look down to make sure I was still human.

When the green flag flew and the cars shot forward, I didn't blink. I couldn't take my eyes off Sterling long enough to blink. He quickly maneuvered his car from the middle of the group to the front. As he raced around the track, dirt flying, I felt as though my lungs would explode. I couldn't breathe as another car clipped the side of Sterling's during the turn and the back of his car fishtailed for a second before he regained control of it. He didn't slow down in the slightest, despite the lack of air in my lungs. Did he didn't know that my bear's overwhelming fear for her mate was threatening to kill me?

By the time the checkered flag flew, there were dots in my front of my eyes and I was holding onto the fence to keep myself upright. I realized I was holding my breath, and forced myself to inhale before I passed out. I watched Sterling safely drive into the winner's circle. He slid his large frame out of his car and pumped his fist in the air as someone ran over to him waving the checkered flag.

Sterling's eyes shot to me and held. His look was pure feral bear as he emitted a low growl. The sound reached my ears even from across the track and I felt a fresh wave of arousal weaken me.

On trembly knees, I turned and stumbled hurriedly to the parking lot, needing some time to get myself together. I had no idea what had just happened. Just as I reached my beat-up Toyota in the parking lot, a fat rain drop hit my face. I lifted my head and noticed the darkening sky for the first time. The wind picked up and I groaned as the clouds opened their floodgates releasing a huge Texas downpour.

I grabbed the door handle and yanked. Nothing. Shielding my eyes, I peered inside the car. Sure enough, there were my keys, on the passenger seat where I'd left them. I ran around the car, trying each handle just to be sure. I was sure. I was locked out.

I'd been so stressed about the interview when I'd pulled into the lot, it stood to reason I'd done something so mindless, but that didn't make me feel any better about it.

I plopped myself on the hood of my car, shrugging as it flexed under my weight. I was already soaked from the hard rain. There was no use trying to find shelter now. I was stuck sitting there until I could find help.

Kyle didn't even know where I was. He hadn't been home when I'd stopped in to change. My phone had been dead, so I'd left it on the charger.

I crossed my arms and closed my eyes. I guessed that, if worse came to worse, I could shift and walk home, but I was not much faster as a bear than I was as a human. I was a hell of a lot clumsier, too.

"Quite the hood ornament you make, Ophelia." Sterling's deep voice teased my senses a second before his masculine scent washed over me.

I looked up, meeting his gaze, and sighed. He looked breathtaking. Rain-dampened hair slicked back, thick eyebrows, his blue-green eyes dancing with enthusiasm. Of course, the man would look edible in the rain.

"Come on, let's get you somewhere dry."

I slid off the hood and shook my head as the dent my ass had left didn't pop back. I glared at it and then looked up at Sterling. He grinned and shrugged. Tucking my wet hair out of my face, I gestured for him to lead the way. I needed the interview, no matter how awkwardly soaking wet I was.

He walked me through the emptying parking lot to his truck. A big trailer was hooked to the back and I realized he'd need to get his car loaded up. I was keeping him from it.

"Do you need to finish up here?"

He nodded while unlocking the passenger door of his truck. He opened it, and before I knew what he was doing, wrapped his hands around my waist and lifted me into the seat. "Hutch is going to help me load the car. I'll be back in just a bit. You stay here."

My skin burned where his hands had been. The feel of his touch lingered on my body. I sucked in a breath at how close he still was and bit my lip. I felt myself slipping and I knew it was bad, but I didn't know how to stop it. I was putty when it came to Sterling, and I'd had a really bad couple of days. Weeks, really. Maybe I didn't have to commit to forever. Maybe, I could just steal one night.

6

OPHELIA

Crazy thoughts raced through my head. Cray-zee. I'd been adamant about staying away from Sterling, who was now driving his racecar across the parking lot toward me. I'd been adamant that complete avoidance was the way to go. I was terrified that if I got too close to him, physically, I'd get emotionally attached to a man who was clearly a womanizer.

That fear was still very much alive, but so was my throbbing neediness in the girlie parts department. The need to be touched by him was overpowering my fear. My bear was screaming for him, and damned if my body didn't agree. The hussy. Wasn't it crazy to keep fighting the desires that were plaguing me? They were only getting stronger. Wouldn't it be better to give in and get him out of my system?

It was a cheap excuse, but I couldn't stop thinking about how nice it would be to be the object of Sterling's attentions for more than the few minutes it normally took before I ran away from him. I felt exhausted from the rollercoaster of emotions that I'd been on. Was it so bad to reward myself with something good? Something to make me *feel* good.

Crap. There had been a very good reason that I hadn't wanted to come tonight. I'd never been good at resisting temptation. That's why my ass wasn't smaller. But, as strong as my craving for sweets was, my craving for Sterling Mallory was that—times ten.

I knew better, yet I couldn't help but throw caution to the wind. Sterling had hurt Kyle in a dick move. He could potentially hurt me —if I let him. I didn't have to let him, though. I could make this night all about me.

I could and I would.

Tonight, I would indulge myself—*just tonight.*

I rubbed my hands down my wet thighs and blew out a rough breath when I realized that I'd already made up my mind. I was going to sleep with Sterling. Tonight. No matter how bad an idea the little angel on my shoulder tried to convince me it was. No matter how bad a sister it made me. I pushed Kyle out of my mind and turned in my seat to watch Sterling load the car onto the trailer.

It was insane. God, so insane. I was going to do it, though.

I rummaged around in my purse for mints and popped two in my mouth before discreetly sniffing my pits to make sure I smelled fresh. All I smelled was rain, so good to go. I'd thrown on an older sundress before coming and it was cute enough. I tugged it up a little on my thighs and said a prayer of thanks for the laser hair removal I'd had done in Nashville.

I tugged my hair out of its ponytail and tried to rake my fingers through it so it would look sexy instead of like a frizzy, wet mop. I had to work without a mirror. I wasn't going to chance Sterling seeing me check myself out while waiting for him. I probably wasn't my prettiest, but he probably didn't care. He didn't seem to have a type, so I'd probably do.

I forced myself to be still and wait while he finished up with the car. He was dripping wet and grinning like a schoolkid when he climbed in.

"Sorry about making you wait." He whipped his hair back and started the truck. "Dang, I should have turned on some heat for you. You're probably cold."

I shook my head and opened my mouth to reply, but I seemed to have lost all ability to speak. I spun my head to look out of my window and mentally slapped myself. Hard.

"Okay, what kind of interview questions do you need to ask?"

Interview. Questions. Shit. I turned back to him with pink cheeks and said the first thing to pop into my head. "Why'd you do what you did to Kyle?"

Double shit. Not what I had meant to ask. Not what I had wanted to bring up at all on the night that I'd just vowed to forget about Kyle so I could selfishly indulge in some raunchy sex.

Sterling coughed and adjusted the vents. "Karen wanted a really personal interview, huh?"

I groaned. "No. I'm supposed to interview you about the race and winning. Forget it."

He turned to me and just stared for a few seconds longer than I was comfortable with. I pushed my dress down and crossed my legs. I was an idiot, both with my diarrhea of the mouth and with my stupid decision to sleep with him.

"No, it's okay. We didn't really talk much last time we were together, did we?"

My face heated and I thought about getting out and walking home. I might salvage a bit of my dignity that way. "No, we didn't."

"John Wayne has healed just fine, thank you. You never checked to see."

I snorted and shifted so I could face him. "John Wayne? No. Forget I asked."

His grin was crooked and sent tingles straight to my core. "You sure? It's a good story."

Maybe sleeping with him was back on the table. "I'm sure. And of course I didn't check on you, Sterling. I don't know the proper protocol after punching someone in the penis, but I'm pretty sure it's not sending get well cards."

"It would've been a polite thing to do."

I laughed and shook my head, sobering up. "A polite thing to do would've been to refrain from sleeping with my brother's fiancée."

He sighed and nodded. "You're right. I fucked up. I can assure you that there's not a single one of my mistakes I regret more—and I've made some doozies."

"Why'd you do it?"

"Fuck, Ophelia." He shifted in his seat and gripped the steering wheel. "Want to go for a ride?"

I glanced over at my car and shrugged. "I locked myself out of my car. So, I guess."

The heaviness faded as he grinned again. His eyes flashed and he put the truck in drive and pulled out of the lot. "I've got to drop the trailer off at Hutch's shop, but then I have something I want to show you."

I watched the road fly by and uncrossed my legs. I noticed his eyes stray to them and my heart beat faster. I knew he could hear it, and that just made the situation that much more intense. I was too far gone. Being alone in the truck with him had been a line. I'd crossed it. That meant that I couldn't go back until I'd completed my mission.

I brushed my hand over my knee and nonchalantly shifted the hem of my dress up a bit. "Where are you taking me?"

"It's a surprise." His voice deepened and I could hear his heartrate increase.

"How did winning feel?" I tried to distract myself, because if I didn't, he was going to know, in just a few seconds, exactly how turned on I was.

"Better with you in the stands." He passed a car that was going too slowly for his liking, and adjusted the heat. "Are you hot? I'm burning up."

I smiled to myself and fanned the neckline of my dress, flashing him hints of cleavage. "It is a little hot in here."

He swerved to miss a downed tree-limb and swore. He remained quiet, but his eyes flitted to me again and again. I slid the hem of my dress up higher and then lifted my hair off of my neck and fanned myself. Pretending I didn't hear his growling, I sighed heavily and trailed my hand down my neck and across my chest.

"I can't wait to get out of this wet dress."

Sterling blew out a breath and jerked the steering wheel to swing the truck into Hutch's parking lot. He scrubbed his hand down his face and looked over at me. "I'll be right back."

I just smiled. I liked seeing him so unnerved and knowing it was because of me. I felt empowered, and knew I was making the right decision. Just for tonight.

7

STERLING

My dick was hard enough to bend steel. I didn't know what was happening in the truck. As I unhitched the trailer, I looked through the back glass at Ophelia. A growl rose in my throat. I was sure she hated me. Was she was toying with me? Flirting? Trying to drive me fucking insane?

I'd thought I was being sly, getting her alone with me, but now I wasn't sure it was such a great idea, after all. My bear was begging to mark her and I wasn't doing well at controlling him. I couldn't stop staring. The few inches of thigh that were showing, the quick flashes of her cleavage. I'd damn near ran us off the road trying to glimpse more of her bare flesh.

I could smell her heat, her neediness, but I knew that didn't mean she wanted *me*. Hell, she still wasn't over what I'd done to her brother. To pretend that she wanted me was wishful thinking to an extreme.

I caught her watching me and swore. I was going to take her to the cave I'd found in the side of the mountain where I lived. It was the place I liked to go when I wanted to be alone, yet for some self-sabotaging reason, I wanted her scent there, in my private sanctuary. She'd probably hate it. It was raining harder. It would be slick with mud. She was in a dress. I was practically a stranger, taking her to a dark cave. Now that I thought about it, it might come across as creepier than I'd originally thought. Then again, this might be my one and only shot.

I finished unhooking the trailer and hopped back into the cab. Drenched, I looked over at her and swore that her dress had gotten even shorter.

"The surprise?"

I nodded. "You mind getting wet again?"

Her eyes flashed, the silver glowing. "Again? As though I haven't stayed dripping wet this whole time."

I had to bite back a groan and force myself to keep my eyes on the road. The whole night was a gift, but hearing things that could be construed as naughty come out of her mouth was enough to supply my spank bank for months.

"When did you start racing?"

Racing? What was that? I tried to clear my brain of the heated images of her body, but it wasn't working. "Eighteen."

"What made you start?"

"I like to go fast." I'd gone stupid.

"Sometimes fast is fun." She bit the tip of her finger and then caught the neckline of her dress and tugged at it. "Sometimes slow is even better, though."

"Fucking hell." I turned onto my road and quickly parked at the edge of the overlook. "I'll come around to get you."

I got out and just stood in the rain for a second, trying to cool down. I couldn't be completely sure that I wasn't imagining it, but she might be teasing me. Shaking my head, I walked around and opened her door.

She slid herself out, her body brushing against mine on the way down. Her sandaled feet slipped in a bit of mud and she grabbed my arm to still herself. Her pupils were dilated and her mouth parted slightly as her fingers flexed on my muscle. "Ooh, I didn't realize you had to work out to be a race car driver."

I wrapped my arm around her waist and helped her down the small embankment that led to the creek. Her skin was hot under my fingers and I wanted to explore the luscious curves I felt hiding under the dress. "I work in Hutch's shop some, too. Plus, being a bear, some things just come naturally."

She snorted. "Maybe for you male bears. A hot physique doesn't come naturally to me."

I resisted the urge to look down at her body. "That's not true," I choked out.

She brushed her hair back and slipped again. With a scowl on her face, she looked up at me and stopped moving. "Where are you taking me? I'm starting to feel like I'm drowning."

I pulled my hat from my back pocket and slid it onto her head before easily scooping her into my arms. It would at least block some of the rain from hitting her face. "It's just up ahead. It'll be drier where we're going, I promise."

She wrapped her arms around my neck and held on tight as I tracked through mud and puddles to get to the cave. As soon as I stepped into the cave, her sharp gasp proved to me that I'd made the right decision.

I put her down and stepped back so I would keep my hands off her. One of the walls was entirely lined in gold. It glistened with a rich glow, even in the semi-darkness of the rainy, moonlit night. "It's pyrite, fool's gold, but it's beautiful."

She walked around, looking at everything around her. "This is amazing!"

I'd set up a few things in the cave. Nothing fancy, but a metal lawn chair and a cooler that I kept beer in. I strolled over to it and popped the lid. "Beer?"

She shook her head and kept her eyes on the wall of gold. "I hate the taste of it."

I put the can I'd grabbed back inside, just in case I found some way to get her to kiss me, and sat in the chair. "Want to do your interview? For real? I know you need it. Karen can be intense when it comes to her rag—uh, *newspaper*."

She turned to me and stared with something close to annoyance on her face. "You really care about that article, huh?"

I frowned and crossed my ankle over my knee. Trying to do anything to keep her from seeing my erection that was growing because of the way her dress clung to her curvy body. "I just want to do whatever helps you."

She turned her back to me. "You brought me to a dark cave just so I could interview you?"

I leaned forward, grinning. "What else were you expecting?"

Throwing up her hands, she stomped towards the front of the cave. The rain whipped in, pelting droplets down the front of her body. She turned back to me and glared. "What's a woman have to do to be noticed around here?" she spat, before stomping off.

I was dumbfounded for a few seconds, but as soon as I heard her small cry, I charged out of the cave, my bear on the verge of a shift at the idea of her hurt. I spotted her on the ground, in a puddle, her dress hiked up around her upper waist as she threw a tantrum.

"This sucks! I can't seem to go a whole day without falling in a puddle! This one is your fault, Sterling Mallory. Here you are putting on this nice guy act, showing me cool places, agreeing to an interview, when all I want right now is for you to be your piggish, womanizing self. Play me, dammit! Or do you not want me? Is my ass too big? Is that it? You don't like chubby girls? Well, I'll have you know that I'm not a huge fan of muscular men...with bedroom eyes...and sexy smiles, so there." She raked her hand through the mud and then threw a handful at me. "But, I'm your mate. You're supposed to want me."

I looked down at the mud on my shirt and then back at her just as another one of her mud balls hit me square in the crotch. I growled. "What's with your aiming at my dick, woman?"

She growled right back at me. "Out of all that I just said, it figures that that's all you'd care about, John frickin' Wayne."

I crossed my arms over my chest, waiting for her tantrum to end so I could grab her and prove just exactly how much I want her. She wasn't content just staying where she was, though. She turned on her hands and knees and started crawling away from me. From where I stood, I could see gigantic, damp, white cotton panties on display, mud splotches and all. Well, that turned my semi into and all out raging hard-on.

8

OPHELIA

Mortified, I was getting the hell out of there as soon as I could crawl far enough to get to a spot where I could regain my footing and stand up. I'd just snapped. He wasn't reacting the way I had expected him to, and I hated that. I knew he was the biggest man-whore in Burden, yet here he was alone with me and... He didn't want me, it seemed. I was going to run home and drink a bottle of wine in the shower before crawling into bed and never leaving it.

What felt like a steel bar wrapped around my waist and then I was hoisted into the air. I slammed into a wall of muscle and I was just about to struggle when I felt Sterling's mouth on my neck. Chills broke out all over my body and I muttered, nearly incoherently. "What are you doing?"

Sterling ran his hand down my stomach and over my thighs. He caught the hem of my dress and yanked, ripping the material straight up the middle. "Proving to you that I want you more than I've ever wanted anything."

I gasped as I looked down at my body, sporting the granny panties I'd worn in an attempt to remind myself to keep what was underneath away from Sterling. I'd forgotten about that. The matching white bra was just as embarrassing and they were both stained dirty from the mud and rain. My bear was urging me to get on with it. She wanted me to turn around and jump Sterling's bones—*bone*. I was a little more reserved, though. While I wanted it, seeing my giant underwear on display like that was mortifying. I'd just gone from sex kitten to frumpy dump in seconds flat.

I pulled away from him and held the sides of my torn dress closed. "I changed my mind. Let's do this some other time. Raincheck?"

His eyes burned bright through the rain. "Is it the underwear?"

Angry that I had just flashed him the awful panties, I put my hands on my hips and glared. "What's wrong with my underwear, Sterling?"

He grinned, slow and steady. "You're still wearing them."

I wanted to stay angry, but I couldn't. My bear was shouting too loudly for me to drop the ego and jump on him. I still kept my dress pulled together, though. "These were supposed to keep me away from you. These underwear had a purpose, dammit."

"They can have a new purpose. If anyone attacks, we can wave them in surrender. Just get over here."

I looked down at my panties and mumbled to them, "You had one job..." I narrowed my eyes. "Hold up, you're saying they're *flag* sized?"

"Jesus, woman! I don't know what size they are. You won't let me see 'em long enough. You want to fight, or you want to come over here and get some lovin'? 'Cause I got a whole lot for ya'."

I thought about it. I kind of wanted to do both. I was feeling feisty.

Sterling shook his head and came at me. He wrapped his arms around me and yanked me into his chest. Before I could argue, he slammed his mouth against mine.

For a first kiss, it was rough and demanding. There was nothing sweet and tender about it, but it was perfect for us. His hands tangled in my hair, tugging as he tilted my head back to deepen the kiss. I wrapped my arms around his waist, feeling the muscles in his back work as he walked us backward. His tongue stroked over my lips and

I opened for him, tasting the rain and something that was purely Sterling.

A moan escaped and he swallowed it while exploring my mouth. As my back hit something hard, his hand stroked from my neck, down to my hips. I felt his fingers slip into the side band of the panties and yank. The material bit into my other hip and inner thigh before snapping and flying off. I tried to pull away to complain, but he followed my mouth, not letting me get away, consuming all of my complaints.

Bare from the waist down, I squeezed my thighs together, trying to ease the tension that was building faster than I could maintain control. I wanted to touch him as much as he was touching me and it was all I could do to not beg him to just take me right there. I stroked my hands under his shirt, under the wet material clinging to him. Moving lower, I slipped both hands into his jeans and cupped his firm ass. His hips bucked forward, rubbing his erection against my lower stomach. Hunger pulsed through me and I wrapped my leg around his, needing him to brush against my core.

His hand locked onto the front of my bra and I felt something sharp brush my chest before the bra fell away, exposing my breasts to his gaze. I looked down to see his hand returning to fingers instead of claws.

I gaped at him. "You can do that?"

He ignored me while drinking in the sight of my chest. He cupped my breasts and groaned when they filled his hands. "Fuck. Your body is a dream, Ophelia."

My head flew back and a cry left my throat as he dropped his mouth and sucked in one of my hardened and sensitive nipples. I dug my fingers into his ass and pulled him into me harder.

His mouth switched to my other nipple and he devoured me, tugging and pulling with his teeth before soothing with his tongue. His hands pushed my shredded dress off my shoulders and went to my ass. He easily lifted me and then pinned me against the rock wall behind us. Rain pelted us, but neither of us noticed as we focused on the sensations of each other.

I wrapped my legs around his waist and tugged on his hair. "I... need you."

His hand slipped below my ass and his fingertips brushed over the folds of my pussy. He growled as I gasped his name and then slid a long, thick finger into me. "So wet and tight for me."

I was a woman lost. My body belonged to him and there was no hope of me ever getting it back in one piece. With one finger, he was more skilled than any man I'd ever been with before. I clenched around him and found his mouth with mine. Kissing him hard, I felt him add another finger. He scissored them in me, stretching me.

Sterling kissed down my chin and throat before nuzzling his mouth against my neck, igniting a fire in my body. Wetness pooled around his fingers and he eased in a third one before curling them and rubbing an untouched spot inside of me.

Stars flashed in front of my eyes as my mouth fell open in a silent cry. I dropped my head to the wall behind me and blinked away raindrops that fell against my face. Pleasure surged through me as he moved his fingers, pumping in and out of me at a maddeningly slow pace, like he didn't have a care in the world, like I wasn't on the verge of dying from the pleasure he was giving me.

"Tell me you want me to take you right here, O. Tell me what you want and how you want it. I want to hear it from your sexy mouth."

I lifted my head and opened my eyes to find him gazing at me with so much intensity that I couldn't do anything but give him what he asked for. "I want you right here, right now, Sterling. I need you. I need you fast and hard and *naked*. Why are you still dressed?"

He pulled his fingers from me and my legs dropped down until I was standing. He stripped his wet clothes off faster than I would've thought possible.

Gloriously naked, looking like some mythical sex god, he strode back to me and grabbed my hair again. This time, when he kissed me, it was a promise that I felt all the way to the tips of my toes. He was just getting started with me.

I didn't know if there was ever any going back.

9

STERLING

Seeing her standing in front of me, naked, here at my cave, hit me like a ton of bricks. *Mine.* Ophelia was *mine.* Why hadn't I been trying harder to make her see that? I just needed to show her what she meant to me. Starting with giving her enough orgasms to send her soaring to the moon. I wanted to make her come harder than she ever had before.

My bear hated the thought of men touching her before us and wanted to brand her, erasing every memory she had of anyone before me. He demanded that I sink my teeth into her neck and mark her. I agreed, but wouldn't dare do it without her permission.

She wasn't ready for that, I was willing to bet. So, I'd keep my teeth to myself. For tonight, anyway.

I picked her up again and, that time, when her legs locked around my waist, it was with my dick trapped against her hot pussy. Her moan was pure seduction and immediately set me teetering on the edge of losing all restraint. I wanted to take my time and be gentle with her, but if she kept moaning like that, there was no telling if I'd be able to maintain control.

"In me. I need you *in* me, Sterling. *Please.*"

That was it. My control withered and snapped. I shifted my hips to line our bodies up. Her head fell backwards and her nails raked down my back as I plunged into her, entering her in one fast stroke. Her body gripped me like a glove. I clenched my jaw and braced one arm on the wall behind her to try to find some semblance of stability while the rest of the world fell away around us.

"Sterling! Yes, please!" Her broken voice cried out to me as her walls pulsed around me, squeezing and releasing, milking me until she damn near had my eyes crossing.

I somehow managed to slide out of her and then pushed back in. Lust dictated the pace and it was fast and hard. I wrapped my arm around her back to keep from hurting her against the rough wall behind her and took her mouth in a kiss that was just as forceful and demanding.

Her hands were all over me, raking and scratching. Her mouth, as sweet as the rest of her, gave as good as she got. She fought me for control of our kiss and let out a wild cry when I lightly bit her bottom lip. "Too good!"

I buried my face against her neck and growled as her scent beckoned me. I wanted to claim her and mark her as my own. I needed it. Taking her flesh between my teeth, I bit, not hard enough to mark her, but enough to let her know what I wanted. Like a switch, she exposed the entire length of her smooth neck to me. Raking my teeth along it, I stopped at the spot my bear chose and sucked hard on it.

Ophelia screamed my name and her body clamped down on my dick as her orgasm hit her. She practically vibrated against me, her wetness flowed out of her.

I was gone. There was no way I could watch my woman come and not follow her right over the edge. I growled and let out a roar as I slammed home in her once more before spilling every drop of my seed into her.

My knees shook. I tightened my hold on her and carried her into the cave. Both of us, naked and wet, panted, gasping for air as I sat down in the chair with her still impaled on me. My dick was somehow still hard and I felt like the life was being sucked from me every time her walls pulsed around me. She was a fucking goddess, this woman. She was...everything.

I leaned back in the chair and pulled her with me until her head rested on my chest. Her hands came up to rest there, too, her fingers lightly running over the dusting of chest hair.

"Was that the mate bond?" She didn't lift her head and I got the feeling that she felt silly asking.

I pressed a kiss to the top of her head and grunted. "Never had a mate before, but that was the most amazing thing I've ever felt, and I give you full credit for that."

She let out a soft giggle that made my dick jerk.

"Calm down, big guy."

"Like that'll ever be possible with you anywhere near."

She sat up, crossing her arm over her chest to hide her bareness. "This is dangerous."

I caught her arm and moved it, taking in the rounded breasts and pink nipples. I moved one arm from behind her to cup her breast and flick my thumb over her nipple. My mouth watered and I leaned forward to flick my tongue over the tip of the other one.

Her breath caught and she rocked her hips over mine. "Sterling... Just tonight. That's as far as we can go with this."

I straightened and flexed my hips to fill her even fuller. "You really still gonna pretend that's an option?"

She braced her hands on my shoulders and rocked again. "You really expect me to believe you're gonna stick around for more than that?"

I lifted her hips in the air and held her there while I thrust into her from below. I held her gaze and nodded. "Hell yeah, I do. Hell yeah, I'm gonna stick around for more than one night. A whole lot more. A lifetime more."

She shook her head, even as she moaned and gave herself over fully to me. "I can't. You know why."

I yanked her body down to mine and held her face in my hand. "We are mates. Don't you know what that means?"

Her body responded to the rougher treatment and she practically purred against me. "Not really."

I caught her wild hair in my hand and tilted her head to the side, exposing her sensitive neck to me. "It means that nature made me for you and you for me. It means that every single fucking part of me wants to sink my teeth into your neck and claim you so the whole world knows we belong to each other. It means that no matter what, no matter how hard you try to pretend otherwise, this connection will always exist between us. We can't run from it. We can't act like strangers. I'm yours. Just as much as you're mine."

She held on desperately to me as I raked my teeth over the spot I wanted to mark. Her fingers dug into my shoulders and she shook as the beginning of an orgasm built in her. I could feel it in the pulsing of her walls.

"I want to put my mark on you. Right here, so the world can see it." I bit the skin and sucked, leaving a mark that would fade after a few days. "This is happening, Ophelia. You came to me tonight, and I don't think I can let you go again."

With a broken cry, she came again, clinging to me and repeating my name over and over.

10

OPHELIA

"What made you start racing? It doesn't seem natural for a bear. I felt like my bear was going to crawl out of my skin just watching you." I was curled in Sterling's arms, knowing that I should've made him take me home. Instead, he'd started a small campfire in the cave with a few twigs and branches he'd found strewn inside. We were snuggled, watching the rain fall outside and the flames quietly dance off the golden walls.

"It was one of the few things I was good at. When I was sixteen, driving a piece of shit beater, I outran a cop. Before he locked me up, he suggested I find an outlet for my aggression. I did." He shifted in the chair and ran his hand over my hair. It had dried into a mass of wild curls that he seemed to love stroking.

"So, you were a bad boy, huh?"

He laughed. "I was...excitable. Hutch was the responsible one, taking over everything after our dad died and our mom fell into a depression. I didn't really have a role to fill. I had a lot of pent up emotions, and no one to notice or care. I didn't know how to behave, so I just went with asshole."

I rested my head against his shoulder and looked over at him. "And you still go with that?"

His other hand was on the curve of my hip and he lightly slapped my ass. "We called a truce while we're in here. This is a cave of sex and good things. Not anger and name-calling."

I grinned and shrugged. "Just curious. The guy in here with me isn't the guy I heard rumors about all over town. I want to know which is the real Sterling Mallory."

My heart raced as he remained quiet. I didn't know what I was really hoping for. If he was the generous guy who'd given me more consecutive orgasms than I'd ever had in my life, I was going to be crushed when I walked out and had to call it quits. If he was the chronic womanizer, I was going to be crushed when I walked out and he didn't think twice about me after I just had the most incredibly memorable night of my life.

"This is me. I mean, at some point, I was that asshole. I can't act like I haven't done shitty things. I slept around, everything was a joke to me, I hurt your brother...well, because I could. Dealing with the consequences of my actions, though, has kind of put things in a whole different perspective for me. You're my mate. I fucked up enough to make my mate think that I wasn't worthy to be with. That kind of hurt runs deep."

I sighed. Shit. I didn't have a clue what I was doing. I'd given in and now... Now, I didn't know if I'd be able to quit him. Already, I felt like an addict. Lying in Sterling's arms was the most I'd felt at home since being back in Burden. I couldn't be with Sterling, though. It wasn't right. I owed Kyle my loyalty. He was the only family I had left. I had to be there for him.

"I'm sorry for what I did to Kyle. Because of you. I'm sorry I hurt your brother. The guy can be a dick, but I fucked up. I should apologize to him, but every time I'm near him, he tries to knock my teeth down my throat, and I'm not sorry enough to let that happen."

I groaned. "He would be so hurt if he knew I was here with you."

Sterling's fingers tangled in my hair and pulled my face around to his. "We're mates. He'll get over it."

I laughed and couldn't help running my fingers over the stubble on his face. "You don't know Kyle. He hates you. He holds grudges.

And he doesn't *understand* mates. Plus, he never wanted to know anything about bears since he didn't get the genetic trait. He was always bitter that his sister was a shifter and he was just human. If only he knew how much I wanted to trade him."

"Why?"

I sat up and looked at him. "Seriously? I turn into a furry bear. Not just a furry bear, but a fat one. Not just a fat, furry bear, but a clumsy fat, furry worthless bear who has no understanding or knowledge of nature or the outdoors. I sprout fur at random times if I'm upset and I break things. It's horrible."

He looked at me like I'd spoken a foreign language. "Ophelia, bears are big. That can't be helped. And your bear isn't worthless. Every cub learns about nature the same way, by exploring. Didn't your parents teach you?"

I shook my head. "My dad wasn't a shifter. Mom was, but she was so worried about upsetting Kyle and Dad all the time that she tried to minimize what being a shifter was actually all about. I never really played outside as a bear. If I had to shift, I'd hide out in my bedroom."

Sterling grunted. "Seems Kyle has always been a dick."

I frowned. "He's my brother, Sterling. He's nice to me. He used to come all the way to Nashville to see me if I was ever having a hard time."

Sterling stood up, setting me on my feet and held my shoulders. "It's been a good night. Let's not talk about Kyle anymore. Can I see your bear?"

I frowned even harder. "No, Sterling, you cannot. She's not cute."

He gave me a stern look. "Let me be the judge of that."

I growled. "Sterling, it's embarrassing. With the exception of the granny panties, I've felt sexy with you all night. I don't want to ruin it by turning into some fat, hairy beast."

He moved away from me and winked before shifting. Suddenly, a huge brown bear was standing in front of me. Sterling's ocean colored eyes stared out at me and he seemed to be grinning. He casually leaned against the cave wall, slipped on a slick rain-splattered rock and fell backwards on his butt.

I doubled over in laughter before I could stop myself. It was hilarious to see such a formidable animal look so silly. When I straightened, I had tears in my eyes. "Fine. I'll shift. Only because you're so foolish, though."

I moved farther away and took a deep breath. I closed my eyes and focused on letting my bear out and within seconds, I was her, standing in all my furry glory in front of Sterling's bear. I fought the urge to cross my paws over my chest. It just felt so weird shifting in front of another person.

I hadn't shown another soul my bear since I was a kid, and even then, it was just my mom.

Sterling came towards me, his eyes taking me in. He threw his head back, and I instantly recognized his loud roar as a happy one as it echoed through the cave. He rubbed his nose against my head and I felt a warmth blossom in my chest that had everything to do with him.

I rubbed against him, too, freer than I could ever remember feeling. I watched as he moved towards the cave entrance and beckoned for me. I shook my head, not wanting to show him how much of a human I still was while in my bear state.

He stepped out in the rain, anyway, stood on his hind legs, and tilted his head back before dropping to all fours. He looked at me over his shoulder, let out playful growl and then took off running.

My bear reacted instantly. Forgetting the usual hang-ups, I dropped to my feet and chased after him. Sliding and falling in the mud, I had no chance of catching him as he bounded into the creek and then turned to face me.

I wanted to laugh, but the sound came out as a choppy growl that he seemed to understand. I turned and ran from him, never before wanting to play like I did now.

Sterling caught me in no time, his big body running into my side and pushing me to the muddy ground. He shifted back to his human form and ran his hands through my fur, petting my side. "You're beautiful."

I shifted back and grinned up at him from where I was lying naked in mud. "We're filthy."

He leaned down and captured my mouth. "You haven't seen nothing yet. Want to get dirtier?"

I did, I really did.

11

STERLING

The sun was coming up over the hills when I dropped her off at the end of her street. I hated not being able to drive her straight to her house and walk her to the door, but she was adamant that Kyle not see us. I didn't know how she planned to keep us a secret. I fully intended to claim her. Unless Kyle left town never to be seen again, he would find out about our mating sooner rather than later.

She looked over at me and bit her lip as a slow smile tilted her full lips. Her eyes sparkled and her skin glowed under splatters of dried mud. "Don't be mad."

I shook my head. "I'm not mad. I'm just already resigned to the fact that this sneaking around isn't going to work. I'm going to claim you, Ophelia Barnes. I won't hide that."

"Don't say that." Her cheeks flushed and the scent of her arousal filled the truck.

I turned the truck off and ran my eyes the length of her body. She wore my mud-stained T-shirt and nothing else. We hadn't been able to find her big underwear. No loss there. "Don't say what? That I'm going to claim you? I am. I'm going to sink my teeth into you right before you explode all over my—"

"Sterling!" Her shout was supposed to be a warning, but it lost its weight when rolled out of her mouth in more of a breathy moan.

I caught the back of her neck and pulled her closer to me. "We'll talk to Kyle together. Explain. Make him understand."

She pressed her hands against my bare chest and groaned. "I can't. You know I can't, Sterling. I'll figure something out. This just has to be our secret for now."

I let her slide away from me and shrugged. "It's a bad idea."

She opened the door and slipped out. The shirt fell down to her knees. "It's the best one I've got right now."

"What happens when this has gone on for six months? Or a year? I'm just supposed to stay hidden in the shadows?"

Her eyes went wide. "Six months or a year? I can't imagine this mate thing will last that long, right? I mean, I'm sure you'll be bored with me sooner than that. In the meantime, we'll figure it out. I'll see you later. I hope you like the article."

I watched, dumbfounded, as she pushed the door shut and then ran down the road toward her house, holding her breasts to her chest to keep them from bouncing. Won't last that long? Was she serious? My chest felt like it was being squeezed in a vice. She still didn't get the mating thing. It hurt like hell that she assumed what we had was temporary, but I didn't know how I was supposed to show her otherwise while she was so dead-set on keeping us a secret.

She had some ridiculous plan to sneak around for covert rendezvous and clandestine trysts and that didn't give us a hell of a lot of time for anything but hot and heavy hook-ups. I knew that with what little time I would get with her, I'd have a hard time using it to talk and get to know more about her. I craved her too much. Fuck. I suppose it was progress in a weird way. It was at least better than the cold shoulder I'd been getting from her, but dammit, it wasn't enough. Tasting her had shattered any hope I'd ever had of living a life without her. The damage was done. She was mine.

I'd just have to figure out a way to show her what she meant to me while trying to keep to her cloak-and-dagger ruse.

I went home and slept for a couple of hours before heading to

Hutch's garage to check on my car. I pulled into the lot and sighed when I saw Hutch standing in front of my trailer with Thorn. My trailer was parked in front of the bay door, at a weird angle that made it hard to move and impossible to get the car off. Hell.

I parked in front of the trailer as best I could and groaned, getting ready for an ass chewing from Hutch.

"Were you fucking drunk when you parked this piece of shit last night? High? Mentally incapable of seeing that you'd blocked every single one of my bays? How the fuck am I supposed to work like this?"

Thorn grinned. "More like horny. You nearly ran me and Allie off the road last night. I saw you with a hot little number in the passenger seat."

Hutch's eyes rolled to the back of his head. "Tell me you didn't."

Thorn rubbed his forehead. "Didn't what? Was she married? Shit, I'm out of the loop. Who was it?"

"Kyle's little sister."

"Kyle Barns?" Thorn roared out a laugh. "Like that asshole doesn't hate us enough as it is."

"You can't keep your dick in check, can you, little brother? Why her? She already did a number on you. Why'd you go back again?"

"Shit! That's right! She punched you in the dick, didn't she?"

I growled. "Could you two shut the fuck up for two seconds. You're pecking like a couple of old hens. Jesus H. Christ."

Hutch gestured towards his shop. "Think I have an excuse to peck, bro."

"What can I say? Allie has Georgia and Veronica over all the time and they peck constantly. I'm becoming one of the gossip girls." Thorn hid his face in his hands in mock shame.

I stared at Thorn. "You done?"

He crossed his arms over his chest and nodded. "Yep. Just realizing how much I sound like a little bitch."

Hutch lifted a shoulder. "No argument here."

Thorn groaned. "Why do girls talk so dang much? And some of the things they talk about." He shuddered. "I've been forced to overhear shit that I never needed to know. Like, ever. By the way, sorry 'bout your genital rash, Hutch."

Hutch snorted a laugh. "Har, har. Regular comedian."

I just stood there listening as they ribbed each other and pretended to commiserate about the negative aspects of having a mate. For once, I didn't feel like my heart was being ripped out of my chest. I just grinned along with them.

Hutch finally noticed and looked over at me. "Why are you doing that?"

"What?"

"That thing with your face. It's almost a smile, if it wasn't so American Psycho."

I reached up and touched my face. "Bullshit. It's just a smile."

Thorn winced. "No, it's creepy, dude. What's going on with you? I feel like you've snapped or something."

"You assholes suck. Worst buddies in the world. I'm going to have to go find Sam and Wyatt, my real friends."

Hutch wrapped his arm around my neck and rubbed my head with his knuckles. "Now who's being a little bitch."

I broke away and shoved him. "I'm gonna bleed you."

Thorn saved him, "What are the chances that Wyatt's mom still has breakfast on the table?"

"Pretty good. Last one there sits in the broken chair." I took off at a run, yanking at my clothes as I went. It'd be faster as a bear. I looked back and saw them right behind me, shoving each other over as they tore their own clothes off. Right before I shifted, I broke the news. "Oh, by the way, Kyle's sister, Ophelia, is my mate."

12

OPHELIA

I was going to kill Sterling. Even though the sex was the best thing in the world, he had to pay. He had the biggest mouth in all of Texas, and that was saying something.

My day had started out great. I walked around all morning in a hazy, post-coital glow after playing in the rain all night with my sexy mate. It didn't get much better. I didn't run into Kyle in the house, so I was able to sneak in without a problem and without lying to him about where I'd been. I wrote a glowing article and turned it in to Karen, who was thrilled with it and with the picture I'd snapped of Sterling. I found a few extra dollars in my pocket and bought an avocado to eat with my lunch. Life was sunshine and roses.

The day started to get a little rocky when I returned home after work and Kyle asked me to go with him to watch a football game that the local guys held behind Thorn Canton's bar. I figured that we wouldn't do much talking while he watched football. It would be safe enough.

Halfway through the game, though, I looked up to see Allie, Georgia, and Veronica staring at me. Georgia crooked her finger motioning for me to join them and my heart began to race. I knew them from the naughty book club and around town, but they'd never beckoned me over like they were doing then. I felt like I was being called to the principal's office.

For some reason, I just knew they knew about me and Sterling. Panic made me shake my head and turn back toward the game. And that was the precise moment when things started to go sideways.

Kyle looked over at me and then past me. "Your friends are waving at you, Philly."

I pretended not to hear him and pointed at the game. "Did you see that?"

He raised his eyebrows. "What's up? You're acting strange."

Georgia's voice came from right beside me. "Hey! Didn't you see us? We girls have some chatting to do."

I turned to face her, giving my back to Kyle. I made a face and shook my head. "We have the thing tonight. I'll find you guys there. Right now, I'm enjoying some time with my brother. *Alone.*"

She made a confused face. "How can you sit here and pretend like you haven't been keeping a huge secret? Come on!"

Kyle perked up. "Secret? What secret?"

Georgia laughed. "Well, I'm sure you already know—"

I stood up and grabbed her. "Gotta go, Kyle. I'll be back shortly."

"What's your deal? You're acting weird." Georgia let me pull her to the very far edge of the grassy area, farthest from my brother. Allie and Veronica slowly made their way over.

"How do you know?" I hissed.

Allie grinned. "About you and Sterling? Congrats, by the way. He might be a little on the wild side, but he's damn hot."

I could hear Thorn's growl from across the bleacher seats and Allie just laughed.

I made a slashing motion across my neck. "Kyle doesn't know! You're not supposed to know either! Who told you?"

They all turned to look at their mates, who were looking sheepish, next to Sterling who was glaring daggers at them.

I threw up my hands and groaned. "I'm going to kill him. This is a disaster."

Sterling's head snapped to mine. He frowned and growled under his breath, but I still heard it.

I growled right back at him and shook my head. "Secret. What doesn't he get about that word?"

Georgia cleared her throat. "Why is it a secret?"

Veronica wagged her finger. "Yeah, and why did you keep it a secret from us? We tell you everything."

Allie nodded. "We really do. Too much. Just last week, Veronica told you that thing about—"

"It's a secret because my brother can't find out. He hates Sterling."

"Kyle hates everyone."

"Yeah, except for himself."

I crossed my arms over my chest. "That's my brother you're talking about."

Georgia grinned. "And we respect that he's your brother. It's the truth, though. Kyle hates everyone. You can't let the fact that he hates Sterling keep you from being with your mate."

"I am with him. I was with my mate all last night."

They all laughed and then leaned in closer. Veronica made a 'go on' motion with her hand. "Well. How was it?"

I looked back at Sterling and felt my face heat as he winked at me and leaned back in his chair, looking cocky and sure of himself. I bit my lip and stifled a laugh. "It was okay."

He sat straight up as his buddies started laughing. Growling, he stood up and started towards me.

I squeaked. "Gotta go, girls. Please, don't mention it to anyone else. I don't want it to get back to Kyle."

They rolled their eyes in unison and shook their heads. Georgia caught my hand. "Come by tonight. We can talk over drinks."

Behind a stomping Sterling, Wyatt threw up his hands.

Georgia laughed. "Apparently, we hang out and talk too much for our men's liking. They prefer to monopolize our time."

Allie mimicked Thorn. "I don't need to hear this shit, Allie. It's making me crazy. I think about ya'll's shit way too much. Please, Allie. Go to Wyatt's."

Wyatt smacked Thorn who tried to act like he had no idea what Allie was talking about. Sterling was closing in on me.

I waved. "See you there. Remember! It's a secret!"

I turned and sprinted past a cluster of guys waiting to get onto the field. Into the woods I went, hoping to find somewhere private. Seeing Sterling all angry and moody had me eager to get him alone. Knowing he was chasing me made me hot and I swallowed down the knowledge that keeping it a secret was only going to work for so long. We were both too revved up, clearly.

I raced through the woods as fast as my clumsiness allowed and found a little grouping of trees that lent itself to privacy. I swept my shirt over my head as soon as I was hidden and yanked my shorts down, the smile on my face cemented there, despite my frustration at the man who rounded the trees and found me.

He stumbled and his eyebrows shot up. "What are you doing?"

I grabbed his shirt and pulled him to me. "Keeping a secret. Take your pants off, big guy."

His growl was low and promising as he grabbed my hips and picked me up. "You invest in skirts and I'll get baggier pants."

I moaned as his mouth immediately went to my neck. "Skirts with no panties. Got it."

13

STERLING

I adjusted myself under the table, trying to hide the constant erection I sported. It'd been a couple of hours since I watched Ophelia run off from me while slipping her shirt back on, but I couldn't get the image out of my head. She'd looked over her shoulder at me with so much promise in her silver eyes that I couldn't help but dream of the next time I got her alone.

But...I didn't know when that would be. My mood quickly threatened to go sour as I thought about the arrangement. No part of me was interested in running around like a teenager hiding from his parents. We were *mates.* Kyle was going to have to get the fuck over it and accept that.

I drained a shot of whiskey. Mood officially turned, I shook my head and grabbed Hutch's shot before he could drink it.

He hit me in the arm and grumbled. "Fucking get your own."

I glared at him. "I don't want to hear any complaints from all of you lucky sons of bitches. None of your mates are making you sneak around like a teenager."

"Like a little pussy is more like it." Thorn grinned. "She's crazy if she thinks she can't keep it hidden from Kyle."

I growled. "One. Don't call me a pussy. Two. Don't call my mate crazy. But, yeah, she's fucking crazy."

"Why don't you just tell Kyle? She'll get over it." Sam shrugged. "She's got to, right?"

The rest of us just stared at him and then laughed. Even in my shitty mood, I couldn't help but laugh at him. "Brother, you've got no clue."

"And you do?"

"Fuck you, Sam," I nodded towards the door. "You want to get your ass handed to you tonight?"

He grinned and shrugged. "Why not? I've got time and nothing to do. I was planning on meeting up with Haley, the Sanders' girl, tonight, but haven't seen her around yet."

I grabbed his shot and threw it back, too. "Alright, let's go."

Thorn looked around and grinned. "Why the hell not. Come on. I'll grab a couple of bottles."

We all headed outside, ready to brawl like idiots. Heading into the woods behind the bar, I groaned as I caught a light whiff of Ophelia still hanging around.

Wyatt slapped my back. "It never gets any easier, man. Might as well take all your frustration out on Sam. He's asking for it."

Sam nodded. "I am literally asking for it. I'm bored as shit. All of you old farts are settling down on me. I don't have anything to do these days."

I just grinned and stripped before shifting. He had no idea how much pent-up frustration I had going on. Not being able to joke away my feelings and behave like a complete asshat, as I usually did, had left me with a lot of emotional build-up. Thank god for good friends to beat the shit out of.

Everyone stripped and shifted, all ready to brawl. It was nothing serious, just shifters letting loose some energy. Sam was like a brother to me. I'd never actually want to hurt him. Brawling was natural and normal for bears, though.

Sam ran at me and grunted when I easily met his force head on and we both toppled sideways. Rolling around on the ground, we fought until we were too tired to do anything else. The others played and fought around us, sometimes running over to growl and nip at us. It was something the five of us had done since we were kids and it was nothing that we wanted our women watching. Male bonding time.

When we'd all tuckered ourselves out, we waded into the creek and shifted back so we could enjoy the bottles of whiskey Thorn brought along. It wasn't until they were bottoms up that we decided we needed to have some different fun.

"I miss my mate." Wyatt strolled out of the water and grabbed his clothes. "Let's go break up their party."

Thorn and Hutch both nodded while laughing. Thorn grabbed his clothes and grinned. "Allie will be annoyed for a while, then we can have makeup sex. It's perfect."

I hesitated for a few seconds and then caved. "I, apparently, am in the middle of a high school love affair that I have to hide. This will be a perfect cover for spending some time with my little mate."

Sam wagged his eyebrows. "I just so happened to know that there are a few single ladies in attendance at their soiree tonight. I'm right behind y'all."

"Hey, Sterling, I forgot to ask. What's it like being mated to another bear?" Wyatt laughed and shook his head. "Not too many female bears around here."

I stepped into my jeans and decided to just carry my shirt. "She's beautiful. Her bear... Fuck. I didn't know my bear could be so happy. She's fun. And clumsy. I get the feeling she doesn't shift much, so watching her is like watching a cub sometimes. She's got issues with it because her parents didn't let her shift much, and never in front of Kyle, I guess. That dickhead just keeps becoming more and more of an asswipe every day."

"That asswipe is going to be family, soon." Hutch shivered. "Thanks for that, by the way."

"I'm happy to deal with him if it means being with my mate. I thought I'd ruined it. I was afraid that I was never going to get a real chance with her. After the whole punch to the dick thing, I gave up."

"Rookie move."

I nodded. "Yeah, it wasn't my best. I'm done with that shit, though. She's mine and I'm not ever giving up on her. She's just going to have to get over it."

Hutch ruffled my hair and grinned. "That's the brother I know. There's no quit in this family."

I rolled my eyes. "Alright, alright. Let's go see what our mates are up to."

We walked through the woods, talking along the way. They were all my brothers. They didn't question anything about why I hadn't told them sooner about Ophelia. They just accepted it. We each had our own burdens to bear and they'd always accepted everything about me, even the not so pretty parts.

I'd had just enough to drink to be honest with myself, and I knew that there were things I needed to discuss with Hutch, man to man. There were things I needed to confess and things I needed to face about myself, too. Things I didn't really want to deal with, but that I had to in order to give Ophelia the best version of myself.

Hutch put his arm around my shoulders and smiled. "Why the long face, brother?"

I shook my head, realizing that it wasn't the time yet. "Just thinking. I'm ready to see my little bear."

He nodded. "Man, I'm glad this is working out for you. You worried me before. You've always had an air of melancholy surrounding you, but not like that day in the garage. You deserve happiness, Sterling. For the punk kid you used to be, you sure turned into a good man."

I looked away, embarrassed by the emotions his words evoked from me. "Thanks, Hutch."

I had to talk to him eventually, but we'd leave things as they were for the moment.

14

OPHELIA

I was a terrible bear. I didn't even hear the guys sneaking up, and I didn't smell Sterling until his bare chest was pressed up against my back. I squeaked and turned around to find him smiling down at me. I could admit that my senses were a little stunted, but I had to blame the glass of wine for the rest of my cluelessness. Even if I'd been better at being a bear, I probably would've let a train sneak up on me with the buzz that I was floating.

Giggling, I gazed up into the warm, smiling eyes of my mate before planting a kiss on his chest. Heat radiated off him and warmed me. His strong arms reached around and lifted me so I could wrap my legs around his waist. "What are you doing here?"

He kissed me, long and slow, his hands wandering down to my ass. "Crashing your party."

I looked around and that's when I noticed for the first time there were other men in the house. Feeling embarrassed, I pushed against Sterling's chest, but he wouldn't put me down. I sighed and slumped into him. "Supposed to be a secret, Sterling."

His fingers dipped lower, brushing over my core through my jeans. "We're going to have to talk about that, but later. It's obvious neither of us are in the mood to talk."

I shook my head and ran my fingers through his short hair. I'd just had him a few hours earlier, but I wanted him again. "Let's go home."

His eyebrows went up. "Home?"

I shrugged. "My house. Kyle is gone. He's away visiting a friend in Dallas tonight."

"You want me to go to your house?"

"It's closer than yours." I rubbed my chest against his and pressed my mouth to his neck. Nibbling him, I felt my body heating up. "Now, Sterling. Unless, of course, you don't want to."

He growled and tightened his hold on me. Addressing the group behind me, he raised his voice. "See y'all."

I laughed as he rushed us out of there. Without either of our vehicles, he carried me all the way across town, through the woods, to my house. I marveled at how strong he was, carrying me with ease, and without breaking a sweat, despite my extra forty or so pounds.

When we got closer, I spoke in what I thought was a whisper until I heard it out loud. "Watch out for Mrs. Cummings. She's a nosy busybody. She sells makeup and is always looking out her front window hoping to spot a potential new customer."

He grinned. "You think she's looking for new customers at midnight?"

I shrugged. "Maybe."

He laughed out loud then and just kept chuckling, even when I slapped my hand over his mouth. He snuck us around to the backdoor and then planted me against it so he could kiss the hell out of me.

I forgot that I was worried about our neighbors and moaned as I arched my back, trying to be closer to him. "Sterling..."

He kissed down my throat and growled. "It's harder and harder to not sink my teeth into your neck, baby."

My hand closed around the doorknob and I twisted it, causing us both to stumble into the house. The door slammed open into the shelf on the wall behind it and something breakable hit the floor and shattered. When Sterling tried to put me down to check it out, I locked my legs around his waist and grunted. "Upstairs."

We took down a picture frame hanging by the stairs and a side table before making it to my room. Kicking the door closed behind us, Sterling tossed me on my childhood bed and laughed when one corner creaked and then dipped towards the floor.

I buried my face in my hands and laughed. "You broke my bed!"

He unbuttoned his pants and gave me a slow grin. "We could do a whole lot more damage to it if you like."

I bit my lip and crawled into the middle of the bed. "This is the first time we've done it in a bed and we broke it. Maybe we should stick to caves and trees."

He shoved his pants down, revealing his delicious body. "I'll buy you a stronger bed."

I shivered and nodded. "Come here. I want to taste you."

"I thought you'd never ask."

"At the risk of sounding like a broken record, I have to say it again. We aren't going to be able to hide this, Ophelia."

I knew he was right. Each time I looked at him, I felt the pull stronger and stronger. It was scary how connected I felt to him already. I kissed his chest and wrapped my leg over his. "I'll talk to Kyle."

Sterling stroked his hands through my hair, catching tangles, and sighed. "I don't want to hide this. It goes against my nature. I want to be able to take you out and show you off as mine. I want to be with you every second I possibly can be. I want what my brother and friends have."

I grinned to myself, ignoring the anxiety I felt at the idea of talking to Kyle. "I never would've taken you for the romantic type."

"I wasn't. And then there was you. Meeting you changed me." He sat up to lean against the headboard and pulled me with him, cradling me between his legs. "I'd always heard that meeting a mate changes a man. It scared the hell out of me because I wasn't too sure what it meant. I wanted a mate, eventually, but my life was easier before."

I cut him a look and crossed my arms over my chest. "So sorry for any complications I've caused."

He ran his big hand up my stomach and chest before lightly capturing my neck and running his thumb over the pulse that was beating erratically there. "Not what I meant. I mean... I used certain behaviors to hide issues that I didn't want to deal with before. I don't want to anymore. Life is different now."

"What things?" I knew. I also knew I didn't want to hear it from him. My bear paced in agitation, annoyed at the idea of any other woman touching him.

"Women. Being a jerk. I made a big joke of everything, instead of dealing with my shit." He cleared his throat and his other hand rubbed a soothing rhythm over my thigh. "This isn't easy to admit to you. I want you to want me, not run away screaming."

I forced down the jealousy and anger and looked back at him. "I'm not running. Talk to me. Why did you need to hide things?"

Sterling frowned and buried his face in my hair. Inhaling deeply, he moaned. "You always smell so good."

I wiggled. "Focus, Sterling."

His fingers curled around my inner thigh and tightened. "You keep wiggling like that and the talking portion of this evening will be over."

"Okay, sorry." I grinned. "Go on."

His slow sigh told me that opening up to me wasn't something he wanted to do—it was something he needed to. "It sounds so stupid."

I turned until I was sitting sideways in his lap and rested my head on his shoulder. "I won't think it's stupid."

"I thought this didn't feel permanent for you. Why do you want to hear this shit?"

I ran my hand over his chest, trying to imagine the idea of never doing it again, the idea of walking away from him. It was impossible. "I just do. Now, get talking."

15

STERLING

I held her close as I brought forth memories of my childhood. "Hutch and my dad were always so close. They used to have these father son excursions. I just stayed behind, usually. It wasn't that they refused to include me or anything. I just didn't fit in with them, I guess. I usually hung out with mom. It sucked, but I'm glad Hutch got that time with Dad."

Ophelia stroked my chest and stared up at me. "Did something happen to him?"

I nodded and took a few seconds to get my thoughts together before continuing. It wasn't that I didn't talk about Dad plenty; it was just still hard to say that he'd died. It still hurt. Over thirty, and I still felt like I'd missed a chance to get to know my own father. I still felt cheated. "Yeah, he died when I was young. Hutch kind of grew up all of a sudden—too fast, and saw it as his duty to provide for our family. He was a damn hard worker. Still is. He got a job pretty much right away and started taking care of me and mom."

"How old was he?"

I gritted my teeth and got ready for the awe in her voice. It was the same awe that everyone's voice held when they found out. Yes, my brother Hutch was amazing. "Fourteen."

She bit her lip and nodded. "What did you do?"

I blinked a few times and furrowed my eyebrows. "What do you mean?"

"I mean what did you do? You were so young. You lost your dad and then your brother took over the role as man of the house. I'm sure it was almost like you lost both of them at the same time."

I realized I'd squeezed my arms around her too tightly and eased up. "I didn't do anything. My mom went into a deep depression for years. Hardly ever got out of bed."

"How did you deal with that?"

I looked down at my mate and thanked the world for sending her to me. "I don't know. I didn't. I made sure mom ate, took care of the house and shit, and other than that, I lazed around and let Hutch do everything. Not much has changed. He still works his ass off and I race cars a couple of times a week for a living."

Her face scrunched together. "You don't really think that."

I looked around her room, looking for anything to steal my attention away from her question.

"Sterling. You were a child. Hutch was, too, but he was older than you. You were a kid trying to survive a rotten situation, I'm sure."

"I don't know. I always thought that maybe Dad knew the difference in us from the start."

"What difference?"

I swallowed. "Hutch is a hard worker, serious, and fucking great man. I'm... Shit, Ophelia, I'm the guy who turns life into one big joke. The fuck-up. Cops, women, a string of jobs that clearly shows I have no idea what I want to do in life."

She sat up and straddled me, grasping my face in her hands. "You can't really see yourself that way, surely."

I grunted, suddenly toeing the line of being way too uncomfortable to keep talking. I wasn't supposed to be scaring my mate away, and yet I'd single handedly turned the discussion to how much of a loser I was.

"If that's not who you are or who you want to be, Sterling, change. I don't think anyone else sees you the way you see yourself, though.

Every time someone in this town mentions your name, they do it with stars in their eyes. You're a great man, too. Except for the whole womanizer thing."

I raised an eyebrow. "That's over."

"You were still doing it a few days ago. I heard you."

One more way I'd fucked up. I took a deep breath and was about to explain that the truth was not as it seemed, and explain the whole ruse to her, when a truck door slammed outside.

Ophelia jumped up and ran over to the window. "Shit! Kyle's home!"

I frowned. "Well, I didn't exactly plan on him finding out this way, but…"

Her eyes went wide and she shook her head. "No way. No fucking way. You have to leave."

My bear growled and I let it out. "You must be kidding."

She shoved my clothes at me and shook her head. "I don't want him to find out this way. I can't do that to him. Dammit, Sterling, hurry."

I stood up, suddenly pissed. Shoving my legs in my pants, I yanked them up and fastened them. "You know what, Ophelia? It really fucking sucks to be kicked out right after I bare my soul to you like that. This can't keep happening. You need to tell him because what we have isn't going away."

She rushed to the door and held the knob. She mouthed an apology, but I was too annoyed to care.

"Guess I'll see you around." I slid open her window, still shaking my head, and climbed down the side of their house before retreating into the woods. My bear didn't like this one fucking bit. It felt like I was running away from Kyle. I was a lot of things, but a coward had never been one of them. My bear didn't like retreat, and I completely agreed.

It also sucked that my mate was choosing another man over us. Brother or not. What we had going—this stealth arrangement—was simply not going to work. I needed more from her. I didn't want to be some dirty secret she hid in shame. It was fucking with me. That was exactly what it felt like, too. She was ashamed of me.

I shifted, shredding my pants, and charged through the woods heading for my truck. I lifted my face to the heavens and let out a frustrated roar.

16

OPHELIA

I winced as I heard the loud, frustrated roar from the woods behind the house. Sterling was pissed, and, if I wasn't mistaken, hurt. The timing was terrible. I hurried to get a robe on and kicked the shirt he'd left behind under the bed. I wanted to punch pillows, but I could hear Kyle rushing up the stairs.

"Ophelia?"

I opened my bedroom door and came out. "You're home early!"

He grabbed my shoulders and looked behind me, scanning my bedroom. "Are you okay? What the fuck happened downstairs?"

I held up my hands and sighed. "I... I came home drunk and stumbled in as a bear. I'm sorry, Kyle. I was going to have everything cleaned up by morning, but you surprised me."

His face changed and he backed away. "You were walking outside —as a bear?"

I nodded. "Through the woods. It's normal."

He rolled his eyes and shoved his hands through his hair. "Nothing fucking normal about it."

I reeled like he'd physically slapped me. In an instant, all of my self-consciousness I'd managed to pretend didn't exist after my tryst in the cave with Sterling came back. "What?"

"Nothing. Jesus. I had a bad fucking night. I'm going to bed. Clean the mess up, would you?" He stormed down the hallway to his room and slammed the door shut behind himself.

I stared after him, finally seeing some of the asshole that everyone else talked about. With tears in my eyes, I locked myself in my room and curled up on my bed. The corner rocked when my weight hit it, still broken from Sterling tossing me onto it earlier.

Shame washed over me as I thought about the size of my bear and Kyle's words. I was a really fat bear. A not so thin human, too. Heavy enough to break the bed.

I grimaced at the thoughts racing through my head and reached under my bed to grab Sterling's shirt. Slipping out of my robe, I pulled the shirt over my head and breathed in his scent, calming myself. Sterling didn't think I was too big or abnormal. He liked my body *and* my bear.

I'd messed things up with him, though. He hadn't tried to hide the annoyance at being kicked out of the house. He wanted to confront the issue and nip it in the bud. He was brave and honest and wanted to be upfront. Why did he think his brother was such a great man, but not himself? That's not what I saw. Not at all.

Growling, I yanked the blanket over my head. I'd somehow managed to land a man who was hot as hell, thought I was sexy and beautiful, wanted me, and talked to me about how he felt. Jackpot! Yet, here I was, fucking it up all over the place. I was pretty sure that there was only so much hiding and sneaking around a man like him was going to put up with before he got sick and tired of it. In fact, he may have reached his limit tonight.

I slept like crap, tossing and turning through nightmares of Sterling walking away from me. It was miserable. I woke up feeling like I'd been through the spin cycle of the washing machine, and crying from an especially raw dream where Sterling rejected me and all my friends shunned me for hurting him.

I threw on some clothes and stumbled downstairs to clean up the mess we'd made the night before. Kyle was already gone, so after I finished, I just sat at the kitchen table with a pot of coffee. I had an article to write that day, but I'd already done the research and completed a couple short interviews with which to compile a few quotes. I could just write it at home and send it to Karen if I wanted.

After an hour of trying, I realized I couldn't. I went to the library instead, and sat in Veronica's office while she led a group of kids in a playful story time. I got the article finished, and it was passable, and then headed towards Sterling's house.

I wanted to apologize and let him know that I was going to tell Kyle. After driving all the way up his driveway, though, he wasn't even there. I went to Hutch's and he told me I'd be able to find Sterling at the track, practicing.

He also gave me a disappointed look that sent me scampering away. I felt guilty enough as it was. I didn't need Hutch's judgement to make it worse.

I parked in the lot and got out. Sterling's truck was there, his trailer empty. There were a few other cars scattered around, but when I got to the track, I found that Sterling was the only driver on it. He sped around the big circle, drifting around curves and sending dirt flying everywhere.

I spied several women sitting in the stands, eating and watching him too. To my dismay, Kyle's ex-fiancée was among them. My bear threatened to appear, but I managed to soothe her enough to keep her contained. Presley Gray was no threat to me. I had to remember that.

Sterling pulled the car to a stop in front of me and slipped out of the window. Instead of coming over to me, he leaned against the hood and crossed his arms over his chest.

I blew out a breath. Yeah, he was still upset with me. I gracelessly crawled over the shortest part of the fence and ended up stumbling and falling in the dirt. I got up quickly though, brushing dirt off my knees.

By the time I got to Sterling, he was grinning and shaking his head. "Even if I wanted to stay mad at you, I couldn't."

I scowled and then grabbed his hat from his head. "You can have this back for a kiss."

His eyes cut to the stands. "You sure? People might see."

I kept my eyes on his, noticing the way the blue-green flecks turned darker. "I don't care."

He grabbed me and spun us around. Dipping me, he laid my back down on the hood of his car, his body wedged against mine. Kissing me hard, his hand slipped down and cupped my ass. "You done hiding me?"

I slipped his hat back on him and nodded. "I'll talk to Kyle tonight. I owe you an apology. And I aim to give it to you. However you want it."

Sterling buried his face against my neck and his tongue stroked out to tease me. "I have a few ideas."

I kissed him again and then pushed at his chest. "Alright, that's enough. We're giving your fan club a little too much of a show."

He glanced over at the group and then grinned down at me. "That was nothing."

"I never thanked you for getting my car back home the other day after I locked the keys inside." I sat up with him and wrapped my arms around his waist. "So, I owe you an apology *and* a thank you."

"And you're sure you're not into giving them a show?"

I nodded. "What are they doing here, anyway?"

He shrugged. "I'm here almost every day, practicing. Sometimes people come to watch. There's a potential sponsor coming to my next race, so I want to be sure I'm ready for it."

And my man really thought he wasn't a hard worker?

"What would a sponsor mean?"

"Bigger races. Races that end in higher monetary awards."

I felt his excitement and smiled. "You'll do great. I won't keep you from your practice, though. I just wanted to find you and apologize."

"Want to do a lap with me?"

I quickly shook my head. "Not a damn chance, you nut job. Bears aren't meant to fly."

"Will I see you tonight?"

I shot him a wink. "I hope so."

17

OPHELIA

I was almost to my car when I heard Presley call out my name. I wanted to pretend like I hadn't heard her, but I wasn't that petty. Even though she had broken my brother's heart. I turned to face her and crossed my arms over my chest.

Her grin was more wince than smile and she held up her hands as she got closer. "I just want to talk to you for a second. Is that okay?"

I nodded without speaking, feeling like I was making a mistake. It would pain Kyle to know that I was having any kind of conversation with his ex, but she'd always been so sweet to me. We'd almost been sisters-in-law, and she looked like she was ready to cry.

"I want to apologize for what happened." She twisted her hands together and stared at her feet. "I feel terrible. I know we weren't best friends or anything, but I still feel like I owe you an explanation."

The last thing I wanted to hear was an explanation about why she'd cheated on my brother and slept with my mate. Just being reminded made me want to smack her. "You don't owe me anything, Presley."

She nodded. "I do. I'm sorry for hurting your brother, but after what he did, I just...I acted out. I made a very bad choice and I regret it. I should've handled things more maturely."

I frowned. "What are you talking about?"

She looked confused. "What do you mean?"

"You said 'after what he did.' What did he do?"

Her eyes filled with tears and she wrapped her arms around herself. "I loved him. No one else ever got it, but I did. Not many people come out to Macon's Edge. When your brother came to see me, he made me feel special. He was kind and sweet and pretended to care about me. I didn't have a clue that he had been seeing another woman in Dallas the whole time. When I found out, I kind of lost it. I went to that bar in Burden and met up with the first guy who looked my way. I just did it to get back at Kyle and it was so stupid and juvenile. Now, he feels like he has a reason to hate Sterling, too."

I think my jaw hit the ground. "Kyle was two-timing you? Cheating?"

She nodded and a tear rolled down her face. "I don't know why he even proposed to me, but I guess the other woman is married and maybe he was trying to use me to create a cover for their adultery. Or maybe he was trying to get back at her for not leaving her husband. I really don't know."

I wrapped my arm around her, despite my bear's grumbling. She was clearly in pain. At my brother's hands. "I'm so sorry, Presley. I had no clue."

She nodded. "I guess he just told everyone that *I* cheated on *him* and said some pretty nasty things about me. I deserved that part of it."

"No, you didn't. I'm going to have a long talk with my brother. I'm sorry for what he did to you. No one deserves that."

She looked back at the track and nodded to where Sterling was bent over the engine of his car. "He's a good one. And you definitely have his full attention."

I resisted the urge to growl. "Why are you here, Presley? Do you have feelings for him after what happened?"

She flashed me a grin and shook her head. "No. Not at all. In fact, I've sworn off men entirely. This is the only place close enough to Macon's Edge that I can escape to, is all."

I smiled back at her and grabbed my keys from my pocket. "I'll make sure that Kyle pays for what he did to you."

With a slight shrug, she turned back towards the track. "No use. It's water under the bridge now."

I watched her go and clenched my teeth. Kyle was proving himself to be the asshole that everyone said he was. It made no sense. I couldn't reconcile the man who came to see me in Nashville with the man who lived with me in Burden. I was going to figure it out, though, and then have the conversation about my mate. It was time to stop hiding.

Kyle was at home when I got back, standing over the kitchen sink, eating a sandwich. He looked up at me and frowned. "What are you doing here?"

Unable to keep the sass out of my voice, I let it fly. "I live here. That going to be a problem?"

His frown deepened. "What's wrong with you?"

"I just ran into Presley."

He scowled and grabbed a beer from the fridge. "And?"

"I've spent the last few months hating Sterling Mallory because I thought he was responsible for breaking your heart. You said he was. You said he stole Presley from you and that you'd never hurt quite so bad, or something equally as dramatic. It wasn't Presley you were hurt over losing, was it? You were cheating on her the whole time. What the hell, Kyle?"

His face burned red and he glared at me. He reminded me a little of a demon. "It's none of your business."

I scoffed. "It really is. I came home because you sounded so depressed. I was so worried about you. You said that Sterling stole your future! I physically assaulted the man for you!"

He rolled his eyes. "I didn't ask you to punch him in the dick. That was just an awesome bonus."

I shook my head and placed my hands on the counter, trying to calm myself down. "I'm being serious, Kyle. Why'd you cheat on her? Why did you play the victim when she decided to give you a taste of your own medicine?"

"This is rich. You're going to lecture me on what I do or don't do now? You're the one stumbling into the house, drunk off your ass, breaking shit."

"Just answer the question, Kyle. I'm having a hard time reconciling the guy who came to visit me in Nashville every time I was struggling with the guy who cheated on his fiancée and then tried to paint her as some kind of whore."

"Well, isn't she?" He drained his beer and shook his head. "Jesus, it's not that big of a deal, O."

Tears pricked my eyes and I tried my best to blink them away. "Not a big deal? What happened to you? What made you like this? I never saw this side of you before, but suddenly it's become blinding."

Kyle slammed his beer into the sink and grabbed my arms. "I think you should go back to Nashville. I don't need you here. I'm fine. Obviously. Go back to Nashville where you act like a normal person and I can handle you."

I withdrew from him and shook my head. "What? What are you talking about?"

He shook me, anger and frustration marring his normally handsome face. "It was easy to be nice to you in Nashville. You acted normal. None of this bear shit. You were just a normal girl who had a normal job and normal problems. I could forget that you're one of *them*."

My mouth fell open and I stared up at him in shock. My mind went blank and I searched desperately for something to say, but my thoughts were jumbled.

"I hate this fucking place, Ophelia. I hate bears. I hate shifters and all the shit that goes with them. I don't want to be around it. You were normal in Nashville. You never shifted or talked about it. You were just a normal sister and it was a nice break from all this shit. Being in Nashville was the best escape. I don't know why I thought you being back here in Burden was a good idea. I guess I thought you'd changed permanently and I could have some normal family around here in this shithole."

I wrestled his arms off of me and moved to the other side of the kitchen. "I am a bear shifter, Kyle. I didn't ask for it. It's just what I am. How can you say you hate that?"

He snorted a laugh. "It's not hard."

18

OPHELIA

My chest ached. Kyle hated an entire part of my nature—one that I was powerless to change. "I'm your sister. Mom was a bear shifter. So many people in this town are shifters. You're saying you hate all of us?"

Kyle shoved his hands through his hair and looked up at the ceiling, like the answers he was looking for might be up there. "I don't *hate* you, O. I didn't hate Mom. She hid that shit, though. It's just not normal. It's weird and I don't understand why you'd want to shift into a big ass bear, anyway. It's not exactly attractive."

My hand flew to my chest like that would help the pain he was causing me. "You can't actually feel that way, Kyle. I know the gene skipped you and Mom thought that might cause some jealousy, but this is a little extreme."

"Jealousy! You think I want to be a freak?!" He laughed and shook his head. "That's the thing with all the shifters in this town. You all think you've been given some great gift. You think you're the best thing ever because you can turn into a fucking bear. When really, you should all be hiding that circus freak show shit."

I shuddered as his words washed over me. It was a nightmare

come true. All the self-consciousness I'd felt my whole life about my bear came roaring to life and all I wanted to do was hide.

Kyle scowled at me and walked to the back door. Yanking it open, he shot a glance back at me. "Maybe you should really think about going back to Nashville. Things could go back to normal and we could pretend like none of this happened."

"Pretend like I'm not a star attraction in a circus freak show?"

He nodded. "Yeah. Until you leave, you can stay here, but don't break anything else, O."

The door slammed behind him and I clutched at my shirt, attempting to get it away from my skin. I felt like I couldn't breathe. My heart throbbed painfully in my chest and I started tingling all over. Panic overwhelmed me until I sank to the floor and pressed my back against the cabinets behind me as hard as I could.

I cried openly, burying my face in my knees. Feeling completely raw and exposed, I just wanted to run away. Running back to Nashville didn't sound like a terrible idea. I could go back to real journalism and with the connections I'd made, it would probably only take a few days to find an apartment.

Sterling's face popped into my mind and refused to budge, though. No, I was staying in Burden. He was my mate. I might lose Kyle, but it felt like I'd already lost him. He hated what I was.

Needing to feel something other than the crushing weight of Kyle's disdain, I ran up the stairs to shower and get ready to see Sterling. I knew he'd be disappointed that I hadn't been able to tell Kyle, but he'd understand. I just needed to see him and let some of the comfort he always gave me soak in. I'd finish dealing with Kyle later.

19

STERLING

Pure excitement tingled through me as I pulled up to The Cave and parked my truck. I got out and straightened my button-down shirt. I'd taken the time to get dressed up for the night. It was the first time I was going out with my woman and it was a big deal. Ophelia had wanted to meet in public, so that meant no more sneaking around. That meant she'd told Kyle.

What the hell was wrong with me? My heart raced and my palms were sweaty. I was as nervous as a virgin on prom night. It suddenly felt real, like she was ready to commit. I still didn't know if she really understood the mate bond, but I had plans to take her back to my place tonight and explain it in graphic detail, complete with examples and demonstrations.

I pushed my way inside and spotted my little bear at the bar. There were already a few empty glasses in front of her and didn't that just make the hair on the back of my neck rise. Something didn't feel right.

I strolled past the guys, offering a wave, and came up behind Ophelia. I grasped her hips and brushed my lips over her hair. "Hey."

She gasped and spun around to face me. For a second, it looked like there were tears in her eyes, but then she smiled and threw herself against my chest. Her arms held on tight and she inhaled deeply. "Sterling."

I smoothed her wild hair and held her head against me. "What's wrong, baby?"

She stayed still for a few more seconds and then pulled away. "Nothing. Sorry, just a bad day. I've had a few drinks while I was waiting on you."

As she slurred her words, I counted the glasses behind her and suppressed a sigh. She was sloshed. Still adorable, though. I leaned down and planted a kiss on her mouth. "Tell me about it."

She shook her head. "Let's not—not right now. Let's have a good night. I just want to be near you."

That time, I did sigh. My bear was agitated and I couldn't soothe him until he knew that our mate was okay. She looked like she'd been crying and I had to assume it was because of Kyle. Anger washed over me at the idea of Kyle saying something to hurt her.

"Is it Kyle? What did he say when you told him?"

She blinked a few times and then motioned to Allie, who was bartending, for another drink. "No."

I sat down next to her and caged her between my knees. "Talk to me, Ophelia."

"That's not how you and I solve our problems." Her grin was crooked and her hand rested on my knee and moved higher. "How about you join me in the bathroom?"

A sting of pain coursed through me at her words. The evening was definitely not going how I'd planned. I shook my head. "I'd rather talk right now."

She pouted and tossed back the drink that Allie had slid her. "Well, I've got to pee, either way. I'll be back in a minute."

I caught her arm and looked her in the eyes. "I'm sorry if Kyle upset you. I wish I could've been there with you, to do it together."

She pulled away from me and shrugged. "It's fine."

I let her go and growled. Something wasn't right. I could feel it in my bones. She wasn't okay, but she was trying to hide it.

Like some sort of prophetic omen, when I glanced back at the rest of the bar, I saw Kyle walk in. He met my eye and his lip curled in response, before he headed for the pool table in the back.

I took a deep breath and stood up. I was going to find out what the guy did or said to upset my mate, whether his sister wanted to clue me in or not. I strode across the bar and stopped a few feet from him.

The girl he met up with looked up at me and grinned flirtatiously. Kyle bristled. "What the fuck do you want?"

"What happen between you and Ophelia? She seems upset."

His scowl deepened. "Why the fuck do you care about my sister?"

I growled. "You might not understand the mate bond, but let me clear it up for you a little. When you have a mate, you care when she's fucking upset. She talked to you and now she's upset. What did you say to hurt her?"

I couldn't have imagined a more perfect visage of horror than the expression that spread over Kyle's face. He turned bright red and his spine stiffened. He looked like he was trying to double in size.

"*What* did you just say?"

Fuck. "*Ophelia*, your sister, my mate, what did you do to hurt her?"

The punch he threw was hard for a human. He must've really put his all into it.

20

STERLING

Kyle's fist split my lip and knocked my head to the side. He didn't hesitate to throw another punch to my kidney. I growled and turned back to him, struggling to keep my bear in check.

"Look, motherfucker, you touch me again and I'm going to do something that pisses your sister off."

He threw another punch that I blocked and then swore at me. "You're a disgusting animal. Keep your freak paws off my sister!"

I shoved him backwards and growled. "Watch your mouth."

Hutch showed up behind me and sent his own warning growl to Kyle before nodding to me. "You sure you want to beat on your mate's brother?"

"Don't call her that. She is not going to mate with some filthy half-breed. You're a disgusting animal. An abomination. You think she's like you, but she's not. She can hide it. She's not going to stay here and live as some vile creature. She's damn sure not going to give birth to more little freaks of nature. She's heading back to Nashville."

I saw red. Hutch's growl from beside me was just as loud as mine. He raised his hands and stepped back. "You deserve this ass beating, boy."

Kyle lunged at me and I swung my fist, connecting with the side of his jaw. He seemed stunned from the blow, but shook it off and came at me again. Without restraint, I picked him up by the front of his shirt and the top of his jeans and threw him across the pool table.

He crashed into a group of chairs and slowly climbed back to his feet, blood dripping from his split lip and fury rolling off him. "Fight me like a man!"

I held out my hands. "You see a bear here?"

He came back at me, his intent clear in his balled-up fists. He tried to swing at me again, but I blocked it and shoved him backwards again. He stumbled into the pool table and tripped over his date's stilettos. Going down to the floor, he screamed.

"She can be normal! Let her! She doesn't have to live like an animal!" He grabbed a pool stick and cracked it over his knee, waving the sharp end around like a lunatic. "The fuck you think you can touch my sister after what you did."

I scented Ophelia heading our way and growled. I turned to her with my arms out, blocking her from inadvertently getting hurt. "Stay back."

A sharp pain struck the back of my head and I went down on one knee. I looked up to see Hutch charging Kyle. I shot to my feet and caught his arm. "Not your fight, brother."

He growled. "He fucking hit you in the back of the head with a pool stick when you were protecting Ophelia. It's my fucking fight now."

I took another hit to the shoulders while trying to get Hutch away from Kyle. Having Ophelia nearer gave me more control over my anger. I wasn't going to let her see me hurt her brother. Much.

I pushed Hutch toward Thorn who grabbed him and held him before turning to Kyle and snatching the pool stick away from him. I threw it away from us and grabbed him by the front of his shirt. Calling on the strength of my bear, I lifted him until his feet left the floor. My fist was jammed against the underside of his chin, making it hard for him to breath.

"You're a real shit stain. Be nicer to your sister. Jesus, just try to be a little bit nice. It would be a huge improvement."

Ophelia appeared at my side, her hands reaching up for my arm. "Put him down, Sterling."

I immediately dropped him and turned to her. I stared down at her and couldn't swallow back the hurt and anger inside. I watched as she rushed to help her brother stand. He leaned heavily on her and glared at me. Seeing her choose that asshole over me was a blow to the gut. Not to mention that she'd lied to me about telling him about us. I suddenly felt hurt and angrier than I'd ever been.

"You lied."

Her eyes jerked to mine and then fell away quickly. "Can we talk about it later?"

I shook my head. "Why not? Everything on your schedule, right?"

"Sterling..." She met my eyes and winced at whatever she saw on my face. No other words came from her, though. She just blinked and remained at her brother's side.

I turned away from her, kicking a chair out of my way and only pausing long enough to grab the bottle of whiskey that Sam was holding out for me. I shoved the door open so hard that I heard the thick wood crack, and then got in my truck. Revving the engine, I burned rubber as I pulled out. A trail of smoke and dust hovered in my wake as I floored the gas pedal.

Speeding towards the track, I turned the radio up as loud as it would go trying to drown out some of the painful thoughts threatening to consume me. I was back to feeling like a reject. I hadn't thought it could get worse than that first night.

She'd waited until we got back to my place to tell me she would never be with someone like me. Then came the infamous dick punch. The punch hadn't hurt as much as her words. None of that hurt as much as right now—I bared my soul wide open to her, willingly giving her everything I had, and she would still walk away from me.

Maybe she wasn't ready for a mate. Maybe she didn't know what she wanted. But, the fact that she could lie to me... It wasn't going to work out that way.

Frustrated, I parked and got out. Sitting on the tailgate, I opened the bottle and took a long pull. I wanted her, but I didn't want to spend every day begging her to be mine. Apparently, the only way she'd been able to show her face with me in public was to get sloshed, it seemed.

"Fuck!" I tugged at my hair and growled. I needed a run. I needed something. Anything.

Tearing off my clothes, I shifted and took off on all fours. I had nowhere to go, but everything to run from.

21

OPHELIA

What had I done?

"I can't believe it. After what he did to me, you let him fuck you!" Kyle was on a rampage. Instantly sober after seeing my brother attack my mate, I was driving him home in his truck. He hadn't faired too well, even after taking cheap shots at Sterling.

I'd messed up so bad. I knew it and I wanted to fix it but I didn't even know how.

"Do you care so little for me? He stole my fiancée! Jesus, O!"

I slammed the truck into park in our driveway and turned it off. I didn't care what Kyle was saying. I was already out of there in my head, running off to find Sterling and try to make it right.

"I know I said you could stay here, but maybe it'd be best if you didn't."

That got my attention. "What?"

He kicked the truck door closed and grunted. "You're leaving anyway. I think you should do it sooner rather than later. I'm just hurt that you'd do this to me, O. I don't want to see you right now."

"So, you're kicking me out?"

He nodded. "You let that animal touch you, knowing what he did to me."

Snapping, I kicked open the front door of the house, breaking the wood. "Oh, get off your high horse, Kyle. He didn't do anything to you. You did it yourself. You've been so nasty to me. The things you said to me aren't things I would say to my worst enemy. You find me disgusting? Fine. I find you pathetic. You're jealous because you're weak compared to the shifters around here. Sterling embarrassed you without even trying. You let that jealousy make you ugly, though. That's on you.

"Mom should've made you deal with it when you were little, instead of forcing *me* to hide. There's nothing wrong with me but there's a whole lot wrong with you. I'll get my stuff and go. I'm not going back to Nashville, though. I'm staying here and I'm going to be who I am—a fucking bear! And I'll be with Sterling, if he'll still have me after tonight. If you decide to stop being such a jackass, Kyle, you come and find me. I love you, but I really don't like you."

I stomped up the stairs to my room and slammed the door shut. With my heart racing, I pulled out my cell and jammed at the buttons until I finally dialed Veronica's number correctly.

She answered immediately. "Holy shit, Ophelia. Are you okay?"

I fought back tears. "Can I stay at your place? Kyle just kicked me out and I need somewhere to go."

"Of course! I've been staying with Hutch, anyway, so it's empty right now. Is there anything else I can do for you?"

A sob escaped. "Does Sterling hate me?"

She sighed. "I don't think it's possible for him to hate you. He did look really hurt, though."

I rifled through the drawers, shoving clothes and other things that I might need into a duffel. I'd get the rest later. "I messed up. I didn't mean to hurt him. I just panicked. I was wrong. So wrong. I have to talk to him."

"Maybe give him tonight to cool down?"

I groaned. "He hates me. I knew it."

"He doesn't hate you, Philly. Hutch went out to talk to him. I'll meet you at my house to let you in. You and I can talk."

"Hutch probably hates me, too."

She sighed. "I'll bring ice cream. You clearly need it. See ya' soon, Ophelia."

I hung up and slipped my bag over my shoulder. Grabbing a few other things I thought I might need along the way, I headed back down the stairs and snatched my car keys out of the bowl on the side table.

Kyle was sitting on the couch in the living room, watching me. "Shit, Ophelia, you don't actually have to leave."

I shook my head to stop whatever else he was going to say. "I do. I need some time away from you. The things you said... You're my brother, the only family I have left. Because of you, I may've just lost my mate. The one man who can make me happy. I'm going to be staying at Veronica's. You don't have to worry about me."

I left before he could say any more horrible things about Sterling, and headed to Veronica's. The drive was short, but I still had to slow down to see through my tears. When I did get there, she was waiting on me a pint of fudge ripple.

"Come, sit and have a good cry, Ophelia." She waved a spoon at me. "You can stuff your face, too. Ice cream calories don't count when you're sad."

I laughed through tears as I sat down next to her and took the spoon. I didn't care if the calories counted or not. I was going to eat until I felt better. "Did you hear the things Kyle said?"

She nodded. "It was ugly."

"Has he said stuff like that before?"

"I don't know. I don't think so. You seem to be a hot button for him."

I sighed. "I didn't tell Kyle about Sterling, but when Sterling asked me if I had, I was drunk and panicked. I led him to believe that Kyle knew. And then, I was just so freaked out by the hatred that Kyle was spewing that I went to him to try to calm him down—shut him up. I could see the hurt on Sterling's face, though. He thinks I chose Kyle over him."

Veronica was quiet for a moment and then looked over at me. "Didn't you? From the very beginning?"

I shook my head and shoved a spoonful of the chocolatey goodness into my mouth. It didn't taste as good as it should've and I groaned. "No. Not on purpose, anyway. I... I guess I did. I just couldn't imagine hurting Kyle when he was supposedly already suffering over Presley."

"You've been rejecting Sterling the whole time. Speaking as someone who was rejected by her own mate for a long time, it's agonizing. It feels a little like you're slowly dying inside."

I dropped the spoon and leaned back on the couch. "You're making me feel worse."

She gave a soft laugh. "I'm sorry, but he's Hutch's brother. That makes him my almost-brother. You've been making the man suffer and, honestly, Sterling doesn't deserve that. He's a really good man, despite the bullpoopy that comes out of his mouth at times. He cares about you. You're crazy if you don't grab him and claim him as your own."

I threw my hands up. "I know! He is amazing! I just... I didn't realize. I figured the whole mate thing would wear off and we'd want different things, eventually. I didn't see a reason to tell Kyle when Sterling and I probably wouldn't last."

"No way, mates are forever."

I glared at her. "I know that. *Now*."

"Then stop messing up." She dug her own spoon into the carton and swallowed a big bite. "Hutch talks to me about things. He thinks Sterling is more sensitive than he lets on. This whole situation has really worried Hutch. He thinks it's hurting Sterling more than anyone realizes. Sterling is good at hiding his feelings under a false bravado."

Guilt turned my face red and I began pacing the living room. "I didn't mean to hurt him. I'm new to all this shifter stuff. I'm learning as I go, despite having been a shifter my whole life. Mom never told me anything. She did everything she could to make sure Kyle and Dad were comfortable and didn't have to face it. She didn't do either of us any favors. Kyle's an ass now and I just rejected my mate because I didn't fully understand what I was doing.

"I was an ass, too. Dammit. I didn't mean to. I wanted him. I *want* him. I was just so afraid of alienating my brother. Turns out that Kyle isn't as protective of me as I thought. I wasted all that time—time I could have used to learn from Sterling about what it meant to be his mate. Instead of denying him."

Veronica nodded. "Methinks you owe him some sexual favors for having to deal with Kyle."

I laughed. "Is that all you ever think about?"

With a nod and a shrug, she stood up and grabbed my shoulders. "You're smart. You'll figure it out. Make it right. You both need each other."

"It's all happening so fast. The feelings, the intensity. Did you never freak out?"

"I don't think so. After a year of being rejected, when Hutch finally starting paying attention to me, I was ready. It is fast and intense, though. That's just the way it works. Mates are soulmates, Ophelia. It's the whole thing. Love at first sight, lust at first sight, can't breathe, can't eat, can't sleep kind of love. The faster you stop digging in your heels, the faster you'll get where you're meant to be."

22

STERLING

Through my drunken stupor, I noticed a bear lumbering towards me. Hutch. I shifted back to human, knowing that he'd want to talk. I sighed. I was sitting on the grass outside of the track, wallowing in my misery.

"You look like hell," he said after shifting back.

I sent Hutch an unamused expression. "Thanks. What are you doing here?"

"Checking on you. Things got ugly tonight." He grabbed the bottle of whiskey and tipped it over, letting the last drop fall out. "You did a number on yourself, huh?"

"We're bears. I'll be sober in an hour."

"Yeah. But right now?"

"Drunk as hell." I chuckled and fell back in the grass, feeling the cool earth beneath my skin. "Did you see her leave?"

"Yeah. She didn't look like she was feeling too hot. There were tears." He grunted. "She's a handful."

I threw my arm over my face, hating the pain I felt at hearing that she'd been crying. "She chose him over me."

"Yeah, but we both know she didn't mean to. She looked horrified and shocked by what was happening."

I sat up and just started talking, letting the liquor loosen my tongue. "Maybe she made the right choice. Maybe I don't measure up. I've never been very good at anything in life, so why would this be any different?"

Hutch remained quiet.

"We both know you got all the positive qualities from Dad. All the good-guy genes. I'm a fucking joke." I scrubbed my hands down my face. "Jesus, she could probably see it a mile away."

Hutch slapped the back of my head. Hard. "What the fuck are you talking like that for?"

"Think about it, Hutch. I think there was a reason Dad never asked me to come along with y'all when you went up the mountain. Or when you went anywhere. I... I'm not like you. You were both hard workers, straight-arrows, serious-minded, and just...good men. You knew what to do when things hit the fan. He chose you for a reason."

Hutch jerked backwards like I'd hit him. "What?"

"I don't know. I have all this turmoil in me, man. I'm struggling. I've been struggling. I feel like a loser. I don't know what I want, where I should go, what I should do. I've just gotten through life by making everything into a colossal joke and trying to be someone I'm not. A grown man, a badass shifter, and sometimes...I...what the fuck is wrong with me?"

Hutch frowned and then shook his head. "Nothing. You're normal, Sterling. I get sad, too, brother. We all do. That's life. Shit happens to everyone. We all just survive the best we can. You've always taken things to heart, though. Dad used to say that about you."

I jerked my eyes to his. "What'd he say?"

"That you felt things deeper than most people. He thought you enjoyed being with Mom more, so he let you have your time with her. I promise you that he wasn't choosing me over you, Sterling. You were just younger and operated differently. He was proud of you—just the way you were."

"I've never been as good as you. With Dad, you did everything right. Then you supported me and Mom. When Mom was heart-broken over losing her mate, and wouldn't come out of her room for days, you took care of us. You did everything you could for us. Shit, you became a man at fourteen and there are days when I still feel like I'm struggling to be a man. I feel so awkward sometimes that all I can do is say the dumbest shit. Or, before Ophelia, not say anything and just sleep with whatever woman would have me to feel like I was doing the normal guy thing."

"Sterling, you're too hard on yourself. What more do you think you should be doing?"

I held up my hands and tipped my head back to look at the sky. "Fuck. I don't know. I could be farther along in my career. I just haven't taken any initiative. The only reason I agreed to talk to this new sponsor was because I was suffocating being in Burden with Ophelia walking around not talking to me."

"You haven't been paying attention. I stopped working as much as I was. I was using it as a crutch to deal with my own issues. I'm fine and the only thing I need from you—is *you*. My brother. You're a good man. Everyone knows it. Veronica is somewhere, right now, lecturing your mate about what a great guy you are. She called you her adopted brother and swore that she was going to get Ophelia in line."

My heart thudded harder in my chest. "I've never felt like I was good enough, Hutch."

"And you've always been wrong. You're awesome, man. The best brother I ever refused to look at for the first month of his life. You really killed my only child gig. Dad would be so fucking angry with himself if he knew that in trying to do the best for you all those years ago, he hurt you like this."

I shrugged and tried to hear what he was saying. "I have shit I have to work out, huh?"

He threw his arm around my shoulders and grunted. "We all have our burdens. Things don't just solve themselves because we find our mates. I still have shit I have to get through. Thorn does, Wyatt does, and lord knows Sam is a wreck. No one is expecting you to be perfect, man. We love you the way you are. Although, I'd like you better if you started being nicer to yourself."

I smiled. "So, Veronica is fighting for me, huh?"

Hutch growled. "There are moments when I wonder if she likes you more than me."

That got a laugh from me. Feeling lighter, I shook my head. "I might've overreacted about Ophelia. He is her brother, after all. Shit, it just feels fucking awful when she goes to his side instead of mine."

"Yeah, having a mate is both the most amazing thing in the world and scariest thing in the world. Knowing that this pint-sized woman has so much power over you is frightening. Veronica could break me in two by saying she doesn't want me—kill me by walking away,.."

"I should go find Ophelia—talk to her."

Hutch stood up and shook his head. "Not what I said."

I frowned. "What do you mean?"

"Your girl has had it easy. She needs to fight for you. Let her do it. You need it, too. Let her show you how much she wants you. It could help with some of those *issues* you need to work on."

"I'm supposed to be heading up to Dallas tomorrow for the race. I was going to ask her to come with me."

Hutch grinned. "Let her work for you, man. Trust me. Let her show you that you deserve it."

I shook my head. "I'm the man. I'm supposed to work for her."

With a laugh and a headshake, he walked back towards my truck. "Veronica's been reading me the riot act about equality and shit. This is a new era, buddy. The women can work for us too sometimes."

I raised my brows at my brother and watched as he shifted to his bear and looked back at me, beckoning me to play. Maybe he was right. It would be nice to know for sure if Ophelia really did want me enough to fight for me.

23

OPHELIA

I tossed and turned all night. I kept hearing Veronica's words over and over again in my head on repeat. Sterling was sensitive and I knew it. He was emotional and, as surprising as it was, it was a beautiful thing. He wanted to talk to me and connect. He wanted *me*. Despite all the shit I'd done to push him away, he still wanted me.

I had to show him that I chose him. He was my mate and I wanted him. He was more important than anything else.

I dressed in a cotton sundress and sandals and tried to capture my unruly hair in a bun before going out to my car and heading toward Sterling's house. It was early, but I was willing to wake him up for what I had to say.

I was done with all the overthinking and bullshit. I just wanted to be with him. My bear wanted to go back to the cave of gold and hide away with him for as long as we could. I wanted the same.

It hadn't been very long, but I missed his touch. I missed everything about him. I wanted to breathe him in and calm the constant panic that had been there since seeing him turn and walk out of the bar.

I parked outside his house and frowned when I didn't see his truck. Where was he? Thinking maybe he'd parked it somewhere else for the night, I went to his door and knocked anyway. When he didn't answer, my stomach knotted. Had he not come home?

It was too early to visit Hutch's garage and I had nowhere else to go, so I went back to Veronica's and made myself drink a cup of coffee on her back porch. I didn't have any story deadlines for the Gazette and I didn't want to bother anyone else so early, so I just sat counting the seconds until I could go see Hutch and find out where my mate was.

In the stillness of the backyard, I couldn't distract myself from thoughts of my brother. I'd have to figure out a way to fix things with him too. My mate came first from now on, but Kyle was still on the list. Even if he'd proven to be a giant ass, he was my only brother. He would have to come around to Sterling and deal with what we were to one another. It made no sense that he continued to hold onto so much hate.

I grabbed my phone and dialed his number, fine with bothering him that early in the morning.

After a few rings, he answered, sounding groggy. "Ophelia?"

I took a deep breath and blew it out slowly. "We're going to talk in a few days after this settles down and we're going to fix this. I'm going to be with Sterling, if he still wants me, and you—you're going to deal with it. You're going to stop being a jerk and go back to being the brother that I love so much. Got it?"

He sighed. "That's a tall order, O."

"Do you love me?"

"Of course, I do."

"If so, it's not that tall an order. I love you, Kyle, but yesterday was awful. I need you to be better than that." I shook my head and grunted. "I also need you to not get yourself killed by insulting a bar full of bear shifters like that. I'll call you in a few days."

I hung up and sat back in my chair. Restless, I decided to walk over to the garage. I'd just sit around and wait if I had to.

I walked slowly and when I arrived, I found that it was still locked up tight. I plopped myself on a bench outside and checked the time on my phone. I groaned. Still half an hour to wait. I was going to be insane by the time anyone arrived.

I pondered the words I was going to say to Sterling when I found him. I went over a speech in my head until I thought I'd perfected it.

The next time I looked at my phone, it was past time for the shop to open. Frustrated, I dialed Veronica's number, telling myself that she wouldn't mind if I woke her up because I was making things right with Sterling and that's what she'd strongly encouraged me to do.

"Hello?"

"Hey! Did I wake you?"

"No, I was forced from my warm bed before the sun even came up this morning. Everything okay?"

I sighed. "No. I can't find Sterling. I want to talk to him, but he's not at home and the garage isn't open today, apparently."

"Shucky-darns! We forgot to put a sign up." She said something to Hutch in the background and then grumbled. "Not my fault. Your fault. Yours and your roaming hands."

I cleared my throat. "Sterling? Do you know where he is?"

She laughed. "Yes."

"Are you going to tell me?"

"No."

I growled. "Veronica. I'm trying to do what you wanted me to do. Now, tell me where he is or I'm going to take scissors to your expensive lingerie drawer."

She gasped. "You wouldn't!"

"I really would. Now, fess up."

"Fine. He's got a big race today outside of Dallas."

I bit my lip. How had I not known that? He was my mate. I should've been paying better attention. Feeling like a heel, I silently vowed to do better. I would be the mate he deserved. "I'm coming."

"That's what I was hoping you'd say. G'won, girl, fight for your man!"

I groaned. "Veronica. Details. I need them."

She laughed. "Be ready by noon. The girls will pick you up."

I wanted to argue but she'd already hung up on me. With nothing left to do, I walked back to her house and set out to find something super sexy to wear. I was definitely going to fight for my man. And if it meant pulling out all the stops to get him back, so be it.

24

STERLING

"Thanks. I'll see you after the race." I shook the hand of Gerald Finnigan, the man who came to observe me on behalf of a big-named sponsor. He'd sought me out before the race to introduce himself.

I waited until he'd gotten to his seat in the stands to turn to Hutch with a grin on my face. "He seems interested."

Hutch laughed. "Of course, he is. You're the best here. And you'll prove that in a few minutes. Are you ready?"

I looked back towards the stands and spotted Veronica waving. I waved back and turned to my brother. "I guess. I wish Ophelia was here. I get what you said last night, but that doesn't mean that it doesn't suck to be here without her. I want to start building a life with her, not play games."

"You're not playing games. You're giving her space—room to show you that she wants you. Trust me, it's what you both need."

I groaned and turned to the track where a group of smaller cars were racing. "I'm just hoping she *does* want me, man."

He looked towards the stands and grinned. "I think you're going to get your answer sooner than you thought."

My stomach squeezed as I followed his gaze and spotted our

friends and their mates, and Sam without a date. Then, even before I saw her, I caught my mate's scent. My breath hitched as I realized how much it meant to me that she'd shown up.

A group of guys parted with a few catcalls and then I spotted her. She was strolling towards me with purpose and a sexy swing of her hips. While I didn't appreciate the catcalls, I got it. She was wearing a little white tank top that left a few inches of stomach showing, a tight black leather miniskirt, and high-heeled shoes. Her hair curled wildly around her pretty face. She was all curves and sex appeal.

My mouth watered as I watched her approach. She put extra sway in her hips and didn't take her eyes off mine as she came at me. She didn't stop until she was mere inches from me. She reached up and wrapped her arms around my neck before pulling me down and planting a kiss on my lips.

Ophelia's mouth was soft and tasted like cupcakes and whiskey as she slipped her tongue into my mouth. With a moan, she pressed her body against mine and ran her fingers through my hair. When she came up for air, her eyes were heavy-lidded and I could smell her arousal. "After you win this race, we'll talk. I owe you an apology—a big one—and I would like to give it to you."

My dick hardened to a point of pain and I grunted as I tried to adjust myself it in the flame-retardant suit. "You came."

She nodded and winked. "And so will you."

Groaning, I grasped her ass and pulled her tighter against my body so she could feel what she was doing to me. "Killing me here."

Her eyes softened and she cupped my face. "I'm sorry I've been messing up. I'll make it up to you, I promise."

I grinned down at her. "You're not going to leave here and try to hide me again?"

She shook her head, and her curls bounced. "Not a chance. I want everyone to know. No more hiding."

"Everyone, huh?"

She tilted her head to the side and bared her neck to me. "Everyone."

My bear growled and I couldn't help spinning her around and

pinning her against my car. I buried my face in her neck and ran my tongue over the spot where I wanted so badly to mark her. "Do you know what you're getting yourself into?"

"Yes. Tonight. After you win."

I threw back my head and let out a ridiculous whoop as I spun her around. "I expect you in the winner's circle as soon as the car stops, baby."

She nodded. "Wherever you want me."

Shit. Right there. I wanted her bent over the hood of my car with everyone watching as I sank my teeth into her neck and claimed her. She was mine. "Tell me, little mate, how much do you want me?"

Ophelia stretched up and rested her lips gently against my ear as she lowered her voice. "More than I've ever wanted anyone or anything. In *every* way. I'm all yours, Sterling."

Hutch called over that I needed to get prepared for my race, but I wasn't ready to let her go. I pulled her against me again and kissed her—both demanding and promising. I wanted to leave her with something to last until we could get out of there.

"I'll see you soon, little bear."

She grinned and brushed her hand over my dick before winking and strutting toward the stands. I watched until she was seated next to Veronica and Allie, making sure the guys whose eyes bugged out as she passed, kept their damn hands to themselves. Knowing we were so close to marking our mate, my bear was feeling especially possessive and predatory.

Hutch came over and clapped me on the back. "Was it worth letting her come to you?"

"Fuck, yes." I grinned and finally tore my eyes away from her. "Come on. I've got more than one reason to hurry this beast across the finish line now."

He laughed and handed me a helmet. "Will we see you after the race?"

I glanced back up at Ophelia and groaned as she crossed and uncrossed her legs. "Nope. As soon as she gets close to me, we're out of here. I'm claiming my mate tonight. Stick around and talk to Gerald, will you?"

"Of course. I'm proud of you, man."

Meeting his eyes, I nodded. "Thanks, Hutch."

I climbed into my car, eager to get to the finish line so I could get my hands back on my mate. She'd taken the initiative. She'd come to me. That was all the proof I needed that we were going to be okay.

25

OPHELIA

My heart threatened to pound right out of my ribcage during the race, and as soon as Sterling's car sailed across the finish line, all the other cars trailing behind, I was flying down the stands. I wanted to see him, but also make sure he was safe. My bear would never get used to it.

Hutch was at a gate beside the track and he grinned at me when I got closer. "Be good to my little brother, Ophelia."

I grinned back and nodded. "I intend to be *very* good."

He let me through and I ran across the track as fast as I could in six-inch heels. Sterling was standing next to his car, in the middle of a crowd, waiting on me. There were people surrounding him, all trying to talk to him, but when he spotted me, he met me halfway and caught me when I jumped into his arms. Wrapping my arms around his neck, I laughed and covered his face with kisses.

"You did it!"

He nodded. "Now, you and I have somewhere to be."

Thoughts of claiming made me blush and I nodded. "Do you have stuff to do here first?"

He carried me to his car and shook his head. "Nothing more

important. Hutch will handle anything that needs handling. We're leaving."

I squeaked as he dropped my body through the passenger window. "Sterling... I don't know about riding in this."

"I want to get out of here as soon as possible, but I've got to do a victory lap. You're stuck in it for now, baby." He crossed to his side and climbed into the car. As soon as he was in, the engine roared to life.

Catching the checkered flag someone passed to him, he grinned at me. "Hang on."

I laughed as he drove back onto the track and then raced around it. Screaming, I couldn't hide the excitement. "Sterling! This is crazy!"

He took the exit from the track and instead of pausing at the gathering group of people waving to him, he stepped on the gas and sent us soaring across the parking lot and onto the highway.

My heartbeat was wildly erratic as we drove away from the track. Anticipating what was coming, feeling the speed and the wind whip through the car, knowing how much he wanted me...it was all exhilarating.

Sterling got off the highway on a little side road and drove up a small forgotten road that was so riddled with potholes it threatened to rip out the bottom of his car. We pulled over behind a tiny house and parked.

"What is this place?"

He grinned before getting out and coming around to help me. "I don't know. Looks abandoned to me."

The house did look abandoned. The yard was grown up around it and where we were parked looked like it could almost be a small jungle.

I laughed as he pulled me from the car. His hands on my sides tickled and I wiggled until he put me down. "What if it isn't abandoned?"

His eyes were wicked as he stalked towards me. For every step I took backward, he took one forwards. "What if it isn't? What if there's someone inside who's going to watch as I take you bent over the hood of my car? What if they watch as I sink my teeth into your shoulder and we both climax like crazy?"

My blood rushed through my body and I was slightly embarrassed by how wet I got from what he was saying. "The hood of your car?"

His grin was nearly feral as my knees hit the bumper and I was suddenly trapped. "I got the image before the race and I haven't been able to stop seeing it. I want you, Ophelia. I want you more than you know."

"Even if someone is watching?"

He continued forward until his chest brushed mine. "Yes. By the time I'm done with you, there's no doubt that they'll know that you're completely mine. Let them watch."

Feeling wild and a little kinky, I pushed myself back on the hood, thankful that it didn't cave in under me, and dragged my hands over my thighs. "You don't mind them seeing your mate spread out like this? Imagine that I was completely naked and someone stood just on the other side of that window. You'd let them watch as you did wicked things to me?"

He growled and dragged me back to him. Shoving his hands in my hair, he caught handfuls of it and lifted me so his mouth could ravage mine. Sucking and licking his way in, he kissed me like a man starving for me, like he needed me more than he needed air.

I found the zipper on his suit and dragged it down so I could get to his body. All I wanted to do was touch him and drive him as crazy as he was driving me.

I shoved it off of his shoulders and dragged his shirt up until I could get my hands on his bare abs. I broke away from his kiss and pushed his shirt up until he got the point and reached behind him to pull it over his head. As soon as his chest was naked, I leaned forward and raked my tongue over one of his flat nipples. Hearing his sharp intake of breath, I gently nipped it with my teeth.

I slid off the hood and sank to my knees in front of him, my hands going to his pants immediately. "Let *John Wayne* loose, Sterling. Now."

He worked down the suit and then helped me pushed his pants down, too. When just his boxers separated us, he growled and caught my hair again. "*Ophelia.*"

I grinned up at him before pushing his boxers down. His hard dick sprang up in front of me and I licked my lips. I'd never enjoyed going down on a guy until Sterling. Something about my mate made it hot as hell and fueled me to try to make it the best blow job he'd ever had.

"I told you I owed you an apology." I took him in my hand and stuck my tongue out, gently tapping the head of his dick.

"Fuck, yes."

I licked the underside from top to bottom and then took him into my mouth, sucking firmly. I stroked him with my tongue while I sucked and pumped the inches that I couldn't get into my mouth with my hand. Looking up at him through my lashes, I moaned as the expression on his face registered. Lust, sure but there was more—adoration...love. A wave of pleasure flooded me when I saw it.

I slid my mouth back until I was just sucking the tip of him like a lollipop. Cupping his balls, I squeezed gently before taking him in again, all the way to the back of my throat. I did it a few more times before Sterling's hands dug into my hair and scalp and pulled me up.

"Enough."

I licked my lips and pouted as he shoved my skirt down to my ankles. "I wanted to finish you off."

He grabbed my shirt, tugging it over my head. "I will let you, I promise, some other time. I want to come inside you this time."

Standing in front of him in a red silky bra and panty set, I cocked a hip out to the side and twirled a strand of my hair. "Want to give them a show?"

Sterling growled and grabbed my waist. "You're overdressed for the show, baby."

I gasped as he snapped the bra from my body and did the same with my panties. Suddenly naked, I put my hands on my hips and frowned. "Those were new."

He tossed them behind him and picked me up, placing me on the warm hood of the car and wedging his body between my thighs. "Don't care."

I leaned back on my elbows and watched as his eyes drank me in. Feeling sassy, I grinned. "Well? Whadda ya' think?"

26

STERLING

Feeling like a man who'd just won the million-dollar lottery, I dropped to my knees and stared up at her. Her core glistened and called to me, begging to be tasted. I kissed my way up her legs, paying special attention to the spot behind her knees that made her moan. When I got to her inner thighs, she shook under me. I wanted to tease her more and make her wait, but I was too on edge. I licked her delicious pussy and growled as she filled my taste buds. Sweet and mine.

Ophelia cried out, running her fingers through my hair, tugging my head to where she wanted it.

I spread her folds with my fingers and found her clit with my tongue. Suctioning my lips around it, my cock jerked as she screamed my name. I slid a finger into her hot center and curled it, stroking the bundle of nerves that I knew set her off.

Her body bucked under me but I kept my mouth on her. Pushing another finger into her, I pumped them in and out of her while my lips and tongue worked her clit.

With a wild scream, she came around my fingers, squeezing them tight. I drank her orgasm. It drove me mad. My vision narrowed and I had to be in her.

I pulled her off the hood and flipped her over so her arms, face, and upper body were pressed against it. I spread her thighs and slid into her in one hard stroke.

Her drawn out moan sent me spiraling. I watched as her hands balled into fists and dragged across the hood as I slammed into her again and again. Her ass cheeks wiggled as I withdrew and thrust back in. I slapped one cheek and then the other, giving in to the animalistic need I felt to possess her completely.

"Sterling! Yes, yes!"

My dick was being squeezed harder and harder as her body milked it, but I refused to come yet. I grabbed her hair and pulled her head up, making her arch her back.

Ophelia's body tightened almost painfully around my dick and she called my name, begging me to give her release—make her come.

With her neck so close to me, I lost it. I let go of her hair and slipped my hand between her thighs to rub her clit. My thumb pressed farther into her and the sensation was wild against my dick in her. I felt her start to orgasm and gave in to my bear's urge to claim her. Leaning forward, I sank my teeth into her neck, marking her as mine. For the rest of our lives.

Ophelia screamed as she came apart beneath me. Her body squeezed my own orgasm out of me. My balls tightened and I thrust into her once more before spilling my seed into her.

Pleasure threatened to take my legs out from under me and I had to lean us forward so the car would hold us up. We both panted as we slowly came down.

I pulled out of her and wrapped my arms around her, holding her to my chest. "Fuck, Ophelia."

She let me support her and looked up at me with a lazy smile on her pretty face. "Sterling."

I pulled my sated body back onto the hood of the car and pulled her up with me. It wasn't the most comfortable place, but I'd just claimed my mate. We were mated.

"You're perfect, baby." I meant it. She *was* perfect. There were things that we both had to work on, my shit and her brother, but she was perfect—for me.

Her eyes filled with tears and she buried her head against my chest. "I almost messed this up. I don't know what I would've done if I'd lost you."

I caught her face and tilted her face up to mine. "It's nothing you have to worry about. It ain't gonna happen. You are mine and I'm yours. Forever. There's no going back."

"I don't want to go back. I want this. I told Kyle that you're my mate and that I'm going to be with you. He and I will have to figure things out eventually, but right now I just want to enjoy you—*us*."

I didn't let the thought of her brother dampen my mood. No matter what he thought, I had his sister in my arms. "If there was someone in that house, baby, you're going to get a reputation."

She blushed and lightly slapped my chest. "Shut up."

I growled and dragged her on top of me. "I want to be in you again. Everywhere. You make me act like a caveman. I want to fill you and never stop."

She moved and rubbed against my already hardening dick. "Sounds good to me. I want everything. You make me so crazy, Sterling. Is it always going to be like this?"

I nodded. "Yeah, little bear. Even when we're old and gray, I'm still going to be chasing this perfect tail around."

She laughed and sat up, baring her breasts to me. Cupping them in her hands, she rocked herself against my dick. "We should stop talking. Plenty of time for that later."

I nodded through a groan. "Sure."

"There really are things we should talk about."

I grabbed her hips and lifted her so I could thrust into her again. "Later. One thing at a time and this is more important right now. We're putting on a show, remember. We wouldn't want some hermit in the house over there to get bored. Don't want him telling people we're lame in the sack."

Her eyes widened and moved to the house, but her walls tightened around me as a fresh wave of wetness coated me. My little mate was kinky.

"Ride me, Ophelia. Show him how much you want me."

As her body rocked against mine, taking us both higher and higher, I took a second to look towards the sky and thanked the heavens for giving me the sexy bear shifter on top of me.

We'd figure out everything else in due time. For tonight, we were going to be as wild as two newly mated shifters could be. The two of us finally being together deserved a celebration.

NEXT BOOK: **Sam**

For more books, please visit:

https://books2read.com/candaceayers

https://lovestruckromance.com

Candace Ayers ♡

Manufactured by Amazon.ca
Acheson, AB

15282976R00072